"Would You Like To Come In?"

"I better not," Ben murmured. "You be a good girl and go inside."

Amelia had a shiver of doubt. Perhaps the wanting was more one-sided than she'd thought. Her upbringing kept her from being too bold.

"Night, Amelia."

Feeling very confused, she watched him leave. Ben didn't make sense, she thought as she closed the door. *Be a good girl,* he'd told her. For the first time in her life, Amelia wondered what it would be like if she weren't quite so *good.*

Dear Reader,

The perfect treat for cool autumn days are nights curled up with a warm, toasty Silhouette Desire novel!

So, be prepared to get swept away by superstar Rebecca Brandewyne's MAN OF THE MONTH, *The Lioness Tamer*, a story of a magnetic corporate giant who takes on a *real* challenge—taming a wild virginal beauty. THE RULEBREAKERS, talented author Leanne Banks's miniseries about three undeniably sexy hunks—a millionaire, a bad boy, a protector—continues with *The Lone Rider Takes a Bride*, when an irresistible rebel introduces passion to a straight-and-narrow lady…and she unexpectedly introduces him to everlasting love. *The Paternity Factor* by Caroline Cross tells the poignant story of a woman who proves her secret love for a brooding man by caring for the baby she *thinks* is his.

Also this month, Desire launches OUTLAW HEARTS, a brand-new miniseries by Cindy Gerard about strong-minded outlaw brothers who can't stop love from stealing their own hearts, in *The Outlaw's Wife*. Maureen Child's gripping miniseries, THE BACHELOR BATTALION, brings readers another sensual, emotional read with *The Non-Commissioned Baby*. And Silhouette has discovered another fantastic talent in debut author Shirley Rogers, one of our WOMEN TO WATCH, with her adorable *Cowboys, Babies and Shotgun Vows*.

Once again, Silhouette Desire offers unforgettable romance by some of the most beloved and gifted authors in the genre. Don't forget to come back next month for more happily-ever-afters!

Regards,

Joan Marlow Golan
Senior Editor, Silhouette Desire

Please address questions and book requests to:
Silhouette Reader Service
U.S.: 3010 Walden Ave., P.O. Box 1325, Buffalo, NY 14269
Canadian: P.O. Box 609, Fort Erie, Ont. L2A 5X3

LEANNE BANKS
THE LONE RIDER TAKES A BRIDE

SILHOUETTE *Desire*

Published by Silhouette Books

America's Publisher of Contemporary Romance

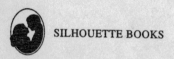

SILHOUETTE BOOKS

ISBN 0-373-76172-4

THE LONE RIDER TAKES A BRIDE

Copyright © 1998 by Leanne Banks

This edition published by arrangement with Harlequin Books S.A.

® and TM are trademarks of Harlequin Books S.A., used under license. Trademarks indicated with ® are registered in the United States Patent and Trademark Office, the Canadian Trade Marks Office and in other countries.

Printed in U.S.A.

Books by Leanne Banks

Silhouette Desire

‡*Ridge: The Avenger* #987
**The Five-Minute Bride* #1058
**The Troublemaker Bride* #1070
**The You-Can't-Make-Me Bride* #1082
†*Millionaire Dad* #1166
†*The Lone Rider Takes a Bride* #1172

‡ Sons and Lovers
* How To Catch a Princess
† The Rulebreakers

Silhouette Special Edition

A Date with Dr. Frankenstein #983
Expectant Father #1028

LEANNE BANKS

is a national number-one bestselling author of romance.
She lives in her native Virginia with her husband and son
and daughter. Recognized for both her sensual and
humorous writing with two Career Achievement Awards
from *Romantic Times* magazine, Leanne likes creating a
story with a few grins, a generous kick of sensuality and
characters who hang around after the book is finished.
Leanne believes romance readers are the best readers in
the world because they understand that love is the great-
est miracle of all. You can write to her at P.O. Box 1442,
Midlothian, VA 23113. An SASE for a reply would be
greatly appreciated.

Special acknowledgments to some very special friends: Donna Kauffman, Janet Evanovich and Susan Connell. Thank you!

This book is dedicated to those who have learned… and continue to learn…if you want to feel more alive, do one thing every day that scares you.

Prologue

Predawn, Sunday morning.

Ben Palmer's face was blackened with camouflage paint, and he was ready for his mission.

"A guy's gotta do what a guy's gotta do," ten-year-old Ben said as he pointed the beam of his flashlight at the graffiti Butch Polnecek had painted on the Bad Boys Club treehouse. Printed in large letters was the plural form of a four-letter word guaranteed to infuriate the calmest male in the world.

WIMPS.

"I still think we should tie him up, drop honey on his face and let the bees sting him to death," Nick said. Nick was probably the most offended member of the club because he was, well, closest to looking like a wimp. Nick was short, skinny and wore glasses, but he had a big guy's spirit. And temper.

"We would get in trouble," Ben told him, and

rubbed some more camouflage paint on Nick's nose. Between his and his older sister Maddie's experiences, he knew a lot about what got kids into trouble. "We want Butch to get into trouble, not us."

"Ben's right," Joey said, straddling his beat-up bike alongside Stan. Joey didn't live on Cherry Lane like the rest of the guys. His parents never seemed to be around. Ben hadn't even ever seen Joey's dad, but Joey was cool, good at math, and he was very careful about staying out of trouble.

Butch was a bully. He was always making fun of the Bad Boys and sneaking into the treehouse. He pounded on Nick every chance he got. He was one of those kids who always did sneaky things like put stink bombs into geeky kids' lockers. But he never got into trouble. The Bad Boys agreed. They hated Butch, and he needed to learn a lesson.

"Okay," Stan, the club leader, said. "Ben will lead through the hedges with his bike, you guys will follow with your bikes, then I'll cover the tracks."

"Then I circle back and leave the gift," Ben said and grinned.

The boys smiled conspiratorially. "Butch's dad is picky about keeping his hedges perfect," Stan said. "Now that he's put Butch in charge of them, Butch will be trimming those bushes instead of going to the pool party today."

"Yep," Joey said, then shot an admiring glance at Ben's bike. "You've got a cool bike. I wish I could get one with monkey bars."

"You should ask your dad to get one for you when he goes on one of his trips," Ben said, wondering why Joey looked sad again. "When we get our driver's licenses, we can all get motorcycles and tattoos."

"Your mom would kill you if you got a tattoo. And your dad will make you drive his station wagon when you get your license," Stan said. "Shoot! Your dad will probably make you wear a suit to the Division of Motor Vehicles."

Ben scowled. His parents had to be the stuffiest people in the neighborhood. His mom was always worried what the neighbors would think. From as far back as he could remember, she combed his hair one way, and he messed it up. She tucked his shirt in. He pulled it out. His father tuned Ben's transistor radio to one station, and Ben tuned it to another. His parents weren't bad, but if that's what life as a grown-up was like, then Ben would just as soon croak.

"The only way you'll find me in a suit is if they're putting me in a coffin," he retorted. "And you watch, when I grow up, I'm not even gonna drive a car. I'm only driving a motorcycle."

"What about when you get a girlfriend?" Stan asked. "Or have kids?"

The thought filled Ben with distaste. "A *girlfriend!*" He shuddered. Girls were pretty, but they did boring stuff like play with dolls. It made little sense to him, but he had to concede that most older cool guys had girlfriends. "Any girlfriend of mine will have to drive her own motorcycle."

"Okay, okay," Stan said. "We've got a job to do. Did everyone get rid of the noisemakers on your bikes?"

The guys double-checked and nodded. "Lead on, Easy Rider," Joey said.

Ben led the way to the back of the Polneceks' yard

and began weaving in and out of the shrubs. Ben loved riding his bike, and everyone agreed he was the best rider in the neighborhood. He could pop wheelies and do long skids without wrecking. His favorite thing in the world was tearing down Snake Road, his hands high in the air, with the wind in his face.

Hearing the sound of snapping branches, he nodded to himself in satisfaction. They didn't want to seriously damage the bushes, just make more work for Butch. Since Mr. Polnecek had been out of town last week, he would get up in a couple of hours and start bellowing at Butch to fix the hedges.

It only took a few minutes, then Stan covered their tracks. "Are you sure it'll work?" he asked.

Ben nodded and pulled the surprise from his pocket. "Yep. Y'all better go. This is guaranteed to last twelve hours. While we're doing cannonballs off the diving board, Butchy boy will be cutting hedges and breathing the aroma of—"

"Rotten eggs," Nick said, pleasure lifting the corners of his mouth.

There were few things Ben hated, but bullies were at the top of the list. Although he broke a few rules every now and then, Ben had a strong sense of justice, even when he was on the receiving end.

Ben waved to the other guys as they left, then lit the high-powered stink bomb. The pungent odor dispersed immediately, and Ben took off like a shot. Mission accomplished. It was almost as good as flying down Snake Road.

One

Ben saw her first, and she didn't look like the kind of woman who frequented the Thunderbird Club on a Friday night.

Instead of tight jeans or a short skirt, she wore a black floral dress with lace at the collar. Her light brown hair was pulled back at the nape of her neck, a few soft curls having escaped. Even from this distance, her skin looked as fine as porcelain.

His mouth quirked. Too fragile for Ben's taste. A century ago this woman would have been wearing a hoop skirt and toting a parasol around her daddy's plantation. That was probably why the beer bottle she sipped from looked decidedly out of place.

Perched on a stool in a dark corner, she put the bottle down on the table next to two others and stared at them as if she hoped they would provide answers.

Ben could have told her beer didn't make much

sense when it talked, but it wasn't a damn bit of his business that an amateur had stepped into the T-bird Club tonight. Alone. Taking a long drink from his own beer, he glanced at her again as the DJ put on a Van Halen tune.

Although an air of sadness clung to her, she was easy on the eyes. The dress didn't conceal the gentle curves of her breasts and hips. Her ankles were delicate enough to make a man want to slide his hands from her feet all the way to the top of her legs. Some men would view her feminine reticence as a challenge. He was a little curious himself, but not enough to do anything about it.

She wouldn't need to leave alone. Ben might have seen her first, but there were others here for the hunt.

Sure enough, not another moment passed before a guy threaded his way through the crowded bar to her table.

She politely shook her head, and the hunter moved on, but another appeared within minutes. She shook her head again and rose from her stool. After waving at another woman, she walked past Ben through the open doorway. He noticed her light, elusive scent because it was so different from the odor of designer colognes and beer that pervaded the bar.

Assuming she'd left, Ben shrugged in approval. She didn't belong here. Out of the corner of his eye, however, he caught sight of her pacing in front of the entrance. The second man who'd pursued her earlier must have noticed, too. He swaggered toward her.

Ben deliberately took a sip of his beer and turned his attention to the crowd in general. It wasn't his turf. He didn't moonlight as a bouncer, tossing troublemakers from bars anymore. He didn't need to.

Nowadays, he had the headaches and joys associated with owning a busy, successful foreign car dealership.

Despite the loud bass, he couldn't help overhearing two voices just outside the door.

"Come back in and dance with me," the hunter said.

"No. I just need some air. Thank you," she said in a drawl as soft as cashmere.

"Let me buy you another beer."

"I've had enough."

"If you want quiet, I could drive you somewhere else."

"No, I—"

"C'mon. You look like you could use a good time, and I'm the man to—"

Ben set down his beer and let out a long sigh as he stepped outside. The hunter kept selling, but Ben looked past the guy's shoulder right into the eyes of the amateur. Wide, blue and weary, her eyes met his, and he felt a rumble inside him that reminded him of his Harley.

Sensing Ben's presence, the hunter turned and looked at him. "You want something?"

Ben moved closer and leaned against the building. "Just air."

The guy frowned. "Do you have to get it here?"

Ben shrugged. "Yeah."

"Listen, we're trying to have a private conversation, so—"

"Am I interrupting?" Ben asked the woman.

She glanced at him carefully, and Ben waited, knowing his appearance didn't inspire trust. He'd been told his hair was too long. He wore an earring. He was fond of his black leather jacket, but even when he wasn't wearing it, the snake tattoo didn't win friends and influence people.

She looked like the type to faint, he thought cryptically.

Instead, she slowly shook her head. "No. You're not interrupting at all."

The hunter briefly paused, then muttered, "Your loss."

The amateur sighed in relief as he left.

"Why don't you go home?" Ben asked.

She hesitated a second, then leaned against the building. "I came with a friend from work and don't want to interrupt her fun." Her lips stretched in a slight smile. "She had good intentions when she invited me."

"But you don't belong here," he said, because it was as clear as mountain water.

She gave a self-deprecating laugh. "No. Not even after three beers." She put her hand to her head. "That was a mistake."

"Sick?"

"Not quite. That's the main reason I came outside."

He looked at her and felt a strange connection. Maybe it was because he didn't really belong at the Thunderbird Club, either, anymore. "You want to walk? There's a quiet neighborhood a couple of streets over."

She met his gaze, assessing him again. "I probably shouldn't. Sherry might wonder if I'm gone too long."

He shrugged. "I can't offer you a ride home unless you want to ride on a motorcycle."

She glanced down at her dress. "I don't think I'm

dressed for it." She cocked her head to one side, thinking for a moment. "You know, I have never ridden a motorcycle," she confessed.

Ben was amused. She whispered the fact as if she were confiding her measurements. His gaze slid over her again. He could guess her measurements. Her body was a nice little package. Perhaps it was good she concealed it in long, flowing dresses, or she could cause a lot of trouble.

"You want to look at it—my motorcycle? Looking won't hurt."

She nodded and gazed at him curiously. "What are you doing here tonight?"

Ben shrugged and led the way to his Harley. "I was bored. I've been keeping some long hours at work lately. I usually take care of my nephew on Friday or Saturday nights, but my sister and brother-in-law took him out of town this weekend."

He would pull out his teeth before he admitted to his sister, Maddie, that he resented not having his buddy to entertain him. Geez, when had he turned into such a recluse. He definitely needed to get out more.

"How old is he, your nephew?"

"Davey's four."

"A handful?"

Ben grinned. "Yeah." He stopped in front of his bike. "Here she is."

"Big, black and I'll bet loud."

He nodded and glanced at her. "I'm Ben."

"Amelia Russell," she said.

"You're not from Roanoke."

"South Carolina. I'm told I have a pronounced Southern drawl."

"It's nice." She was looking at his bike and he saw the wary fascination in her eyes.

"You can touch it. It won't bite."

She slid a sideways glance at him. "Is that what they all say?"

A gentle joke, almost flirting. He suspected it was rare. Ben felt a surprising rush. He watched her tentatively touch the handle.

"How long have you owned it?"

"This one two years."

She skimmed her hand over the side, and he felt an unsettling sensation in his gut. "You've had others?"

"Since I first got my license, a motorcycle is pretty much the only vehicle I drive."

She stared at him. "You've never owned a car?"

"I finally bought one two years ago, but I don't drive it very often." Ben remembered the vow he'd made as a kid on Cherry Lane. He hadn't stuck to motorcycles because of that vow. They just suited him.

"What about the rain?"

"I get wet or I wear a plastic raincoat."

"And snow?"

"That's a little more tricky," he conceded with a grin.

She skimmed her hand over the long seat and looked as if she were exploring something forbidden. "Would you mind starting it?"

The request felt sexual to him, though he knew she didn't intend it that way. "No, I don't mind." Pulling out his key, he mounted the bike and started the engine. "You want to sit on it?"

She hesitated, reluctance darkening her eyes, then

a tiny light of adventure flickered to life. "You're sure it's okay?"

He nodded and helped her onto the seat. She sat on the vibrating bike for a moment, then looked at him and smiled. A real smile. He hadn't seen it before, and damn if he didn't like it. The expression was part wonder, part siren, and it affected him more than every blatant come-on he'd ever received.

"Does it jiggle this much when you ride it?" she asked above the sound of the engine.

He shook his head. "No. You feel like you're riding the wind."

She was tempted. He could tell.

"I have two helmets."

"I shouldn't."

"We could stick to the road beside the parking lot."

She paused, looking longingly at the bike.

Ben resisted the urge to sell. She'd had enough of that tonight.

She looked at the nearby road. "We can stay on that road? We won't go anywhere else?"

"Nowhere else," he assured her, and felt her assessing him again. He sensed she was more concerned about him than the motorcycle. "Is it the jacket or the hair?"

She blinked, and her cheeks bloomed with color. "I'm not sure. You're not like the other men in there tonight."

But he could be and had been at other times. He could have hunted her, but her fragility made him careful. Again, he chose not to push.

She glanced at the bike, then back to him, and

smiled self-consciously. "Can you take me for a little *slow* ride?"

Ignoring his baser instincts, Ben nodded. He put the helmet on her head. "Scoot back and hold on," he said, then mounted the seat.

She pulled her dress up to her knees to keep it from getting tangled, then tentatively put her hands on his ribs.

Ben grinned to himself. When he gave a little jerk forward, she wrapped her arms around him and plastered herself to his back. Her breasts pressed against him, her tastefully manicured hands clinging to him, her thighs bracketing his, made him think of a different ride. She would be nude, straddling him, her eyes filled with that light of adventure, her breasts sliding against his chest while he directed her hips over him. The image made him hard.

Groaning, he sucked in a quick breath and gave the lady what she wanted, a little slow ride. He buzzed up and down the street a couple of times, then parked the bike again.

"It's wonderful," she said, excitement making her breathless. "It was so much fun. Thank you." She laughed. "I feel like a kid. I want to go again."

"I could drive you home," he offered.

Her eyes widened and a long silence followed. "Oh, Lord, I must be crazy," she finally whispered.

"Why?"

"Because I'm considering it."

"You should tell your friend," he said, driving toward the door of the T-bird Club. "Give her my name—Ben Palmer," he said, and helped her off after he rose from the bike. He pulled off her helmet and resisted the urge to touch her mussed hair. It looked soft. Her eyes were glowing with something that edged toward recklessness. He would need to be careful with her. "Are you sure?"

"No, but I'm going to do it, anyway," she said, and dashed into the club. A couple of moments later she reappeared and immediately extended her hand for the helmet.

"Did you talk to your friend?"

"Yes. Can we go?"

She was in a rush, running from something. He wondered what. At a different time, maybe he would ask. "Where do you live?"

She told him as she joined him on the bike again.

He shifted so that he could look at her. "You want to go the most direct route, or do you want to go the long way?"

Amelia closed her eyes as if she were battling caution. "How many traffic accidents have you been in?"

"None in three years. Too many before that."

"You grew up?"

He grinned. "I fought it. I'll be careful," he told her.

She gave a long sigh. "I can't believe I'm doing this," she murmured to herself and opened her eyes. "The long way."

He nodded in approval. "You only live once."

Her eyes darkened with emotion. "I know," she said.

More questions bumped through him, but he put them off for another time and decided to give Miss Amelia a ride that was long overdue.

They rode for a long time, and Amelia loved every minute. The wind almost seemed to blow her sadness away. It was better than a ride at Disney World because it didn't end. The ride went on and on.

Her head and heart were lighter. She felt as if the boundaries had been pushed back. The sense of freedom was heady. At the moment her only solid, stabilizing forces were the powerful, vibrating machine beneath her and the powerful, perfectly balanced man who was taking her for the ride of her life.

She inhaled his musky scent and melded herself with the strength of his back and body. She could count his ribs with her fingertips and feel the beat of his heart against her palm. The wind chilled her, and she would have been much colder if he weren't so warm. Her breasts meshed with his back. His buttocks were snugly cradled intimately against her parted inner thighs. It was shocking and crazy, but her body was buzzing. This was the closest she'd been to a man in a year.

For the past hour, she hadn't been a widow anymore, or a history professor at a liberal arts college. For the first time in too long, her primary feeling wasn't one of loss or emptiness. She felt excited, almost giddy, and Amelia was the most sober person she knew. Painfully practical and conservative, she never made ripples, let alone waves.

The beer and the ride freed her imagination. In another time, Ben could have been an outlaw taking her away on his black stallion. The breakneck pace on dark country roads would force her to cling to him. Fear and excitement would make her breathless. In her fantasy, was he kidnapping her or rescuing her?

Seeing her neighborhood come into view, she was rudely snapped back to reality. Her stomach clenched and she wished the ride wouldn't end. He turned the corner, then stopped in front of her house. After he killed the engine, they sat there in the silence for several moments. Ben removed his helmet. "You still there?"

Amelia cleared her throat. "I'm numb."

He chuckled, and the sound vibrated throughout her. Dismounting the bike, he held it steady and looked at her. "Is that good or bad?"

"I don't know, but the ride was great."

His lips twitched as he gently removed her helmet. Taking her hand, he helped her from the bike, and Amelia mentally directed her legs to support her. Her knees buckled.

Embarrassed, dismayed, she instinctively reached for Ben. "Oh, for heaven's—"

"Weak in the knees?" he muttered, amusement threading his voice. "I'm flattered."

"It's not you," she said immediately. His comment was too close to the truth. Her cheeks heated. "My legs aren't used to the bike."

"It was a joke, Amelia."

Clutching his arms, entirely too relieved that he was holding her, she took a deep breath and met his gaze. His eyes were honest and gentle, at odds with the earring and long hair. If he'd lived in another time, he would have been an outlaw with heart.

"Oh," she managed. *How profound,* she thought and would have kicked herself if her legs hadn't felt like spaghetti.

"Hold on. I'll walk you to your door," he told her and led her to the small porch.

He was being incredibly kind, and she was still trying to clear her head. She managed to produce the key and insert it into the lock. "Coffee," she said, remembering her manners when she pushed open the door. "Would you like some coffee?"

Ben shook his head. "No. I—"

"Or lemonade. I have some iced tea, and maybe some wine—"

"It's okay. I'm heading home."

Finally able to stand on her own two feet, Amelia felt a rush of overwhelming emotions. He'd taken her away from her sadness, and now she didn't know what to do with herself. "I need to thank you," she told him, but it sounded lame. "I haven't felt like this in a long time."

"Like what?" he asked, his dark eyes glinting with humor. "Numb?"

"No. Alive." She shook her head and resolved never to drink three beers again. She felt emotional and impulsive, and all kinds of reckless thoughts were swimming in her head.

Amelia didn't know if it was the beer, the ride or Ben Palmer's combination of danger and gentleness that pushed her over the line. It could have been that tonight was the anniversary of the accident that had killed her husband and left her among the living. Ben's words kept flowing through her head. *You only live once.*

Her spirit chafed at too many days of living too carefully. She leaned forward and kissed the corner of his lips. "Would you please kidnap me again?"

Two

"**Y**ou look different today," Sherry Kiggins said, scrutinizing Amelia the next morning.

Amelia *felt* different. She'd woken up ready to stop wearing black. She felt as if she'd been stuck in a cave and had inhaled a first breath of air so fresh it made her dizzy. "Thank you," she said with a secret smile as she sat down for the morning faculty meeting.

Sherry's eyes widened speculatively. "You didn't do anything you shouldn't with that man you met last night, did you?"

"All I did was go for a ride." Amelia sighed. Her memory of the evening was like a soft-focused picture, smudged around the edges.

"A *ride?*" Sherry asked with raised eyebrows.

"On his motorcycle," Amelia clarified, and put a lid on the fantasies she'd woven while riding on the back of Ben's bike. She was safe. No one knew about those except her. "It was fun."

"I'm all for you having some fun, but I got the goods on Ben Palmer after you left last night," Sherry told her. "He's been in a few minor scrapes with the law, is declared untamable by the women who know him. Plus," she added, "he used to be a *bouncer*. He's not your type."

Digesting the new information about Ben, she noticed the rest of Salem College's teaching staff enter the room. Amelia thought of her former husband and felt a wave of conflicting emotions. "When I told him I was a professor, he told me he owned a foreign car dealership," she murmured, then shot Sherry a wary glance. "I didn't know I had a type."

"Sure you do," Sherry said decisively. "Your best match would be a well-educated, politically conservative, easygoing man who invests in blue-chip stocks, balances his checkbook once a week, enjoys classical music and isn't whiny about sex."

Amelia blinked. "Where did you get that list? It sounds like 'Mr. Rogers.'"

"I got a free romance computer analysis CD ROM in the mail the other day," Sherry said with a grin.

Amelia stifled a sigh. Sherry's specialty was computer science. "If your analysis is correct, then why on earth did you drag me to the Thunderbird Club last night?" Amelia asked, then lowered her voice when she noticed several people glancing at her. "I wasn't going to find that kind of man at that place."

Sherry sobered. "Last night wasn't about serious looking. You needed a change. In computerese, we would say you needed rebooting."

Rebooting. Amelia mentally shook her head. In less

than two hours Ben Palmer had turned her upside down and inside out. That left rebooting in the dust.

Untamable, in trouble with the law, a bouncer.

Amelia took a second, third and fourth look at her outing with Ben Palmer and decided not to go back to the Thunderbird Club.

Every time she thought about that night she got a rush, but Amelia had been raised by sensible and cautious parents to be a sensible and cautious woman. It was true that one only lived once, but if one wanted to live long, she reasoned, it helped to live within some boundaries.

Returning to her previous routine, she ate a light dinner, graded papers and did needlework while she watched the news. To fill the silence after she turned off the television, she played the classical music CDs her former husband, Charles, had selected and waited for the music to work its soothing magic.

She wanted to climb the walls.

It meant nothing, she told herself. If she was a little more restless now, then she just needed more exercise. She should investigate the gym at the college.

The thought taunted her that her mother led a more exciting life than she did. Irritated, she quickly dismissed it.

She couldn't, however, escape the itch to do something different. Her husband had been her best friend since childhood, and she had spent her life becoming the woman she'd thought would please him most. Her discreet choice of clothing, the way she decorated her home, the conservative financial investments she made, even her fingernail polish, reflected Charles.

On one of those endless nights Amelia put down

her needlework, looked at her clear fingernail polish and frowned. How would hot pink look? Disgusted with her craziness, she groaned. Why wasn't the status quo good enough for her anymore? Why was she so unsatisfied? Surely a ride on a motorcycle couldn't affect her so much.

By now she had concluded Ben Palmer had enough sense to ignore the insane request of a tipsy history professor, and she assured herself she was relieved.

Until she heard the distinctive buzz of a motorcycle on her street.

Her heart rebooted.

She heard the roar come to a stop in her driveway, and she held her breath. What was she going to do with him? The doorbell rang, and her brain jammed. She stood, panicked, staring at the door.

The doorbell rang again, and Amelia went to the door. Glancing through the peekhole, she saw Ben and tried to collect herself. When the doorbell rang once more, she jerked open the door, but couldn't squeak out a word when she looked up at Ben.

Clad in a black leather jacket and well-fitting jeans, he looked her over, his hot glance making her feel like she'd just spent too much time in the sun. "You made me an offer I couldn't refuse," he said with a wicked grin of amusement that should have come with a disclaimer.

Amelia swallowed and carefully folded her hands together to keep from fidgeting. He looked taller than he had before. He looked bigger. He looked badder. "My offer," she echoed.

He leaned closer and she caught his clean, musky scent as she took a quick breath. His scent reminded her of the wind on her face as they had driven through the night.

"To kidnap you," he told her. "You asked me to please kidnap you."

Amelia's stomach dipped. How did he make kidnapping sound better than a hot-fudge sundae? She bit her lip. "I did say that, didn't I? It's amazing what three beers can do, isn't it?" she murmured under her breath, then cleared her throat. "Let me get you a soda," she said, seizing the opportunity to run to the kitchen.

She opened the refrigerator door and stuck her face inside, hoping the cold air would clear her muddled mind. Several seconds later she pulled out the drink and took it to him.

"I wasn't myself that night," Amelia began.

"Who were you then?" he asked, leaning against the wall.

Disconcerted, she hesitated. "I...um, I'm not usually that impulsive. I'm much more levelheaded."

"Uh-huh." He took a long drink from the soda.

Mesmerized by the sight of his strong neck and throat as he swallowed, she tried not to stare. He licked his lips, and she remembered brushing her mouth against the corner of his. The thought made her heart jump.

His gaze met and held hers. "You're almost dressed for a kidnapping. All you need are a jacket and some shoes."

He might as well have had *dangerous* stamped on him, yet something about him made her trust him. Torn, Amelia bit her lip and tried to think. "I'm not sure this is a good night for kidnapping."

He arched an eyebrow. "Need a full moon?"

Need courage, Amelia thought—or insanity. "I just think—" She broke off when he stepped closer and touched a wayward strand of her hair.

"Do you regret riding with me the other night?"

"No," she said immediately. "It was wonderful."

He searched her gaze and pulled his hand back. "You're just not sure you want to repeat it."

Amelia felt a terrible tightening in her stomach, but she couldn't deny her uncertainty to him. She'd closed herself off from living and feeling for so long that she felt like a green freshman.

Ben must have read her face. He stood there a moment longer as if he were giving her time to change her mind, and Amelia felt every second of that moment tick inside her. She closed her eyes in indecision, and when she opened them, he was gone.

Ben was in the mood to throw a wrench through his office window. The customers were cranky, his mechanics were irritable, the salesmen were whiny, and though Ben didn't want to admit it, he felt cranky himself. The reason he was cranky made him give the wrench on his desk a second glance.

Of all things, he was in a bad mood over a *woman*, one who wasn't his speed and never would be. Ben had been friends with many women, and lovers with a few, but he'd never spent his days and nights in angst over any female in his life, unless he counted the time his then girlfriend wrecked his bike.

Women wanted commitment and marriage. They wanted a man who fit a narrow mold of respectability. The very idea of trying to wedge himself into that mold made him feel suffocated, so Ben made a policy to never get too worked up over women.

In particular, he steered clear of any woman who wore a business suit or had too many letters of the alphabet after her name representing advanced degrees. These were neon signs that his world wouldn't operate in the same solar system as hers. The one time he'd gotten involved with such a woman his ego had been dented. But never his heart, of course.

Ben had learned women were a mysterious, sometimes pleasurable and always temporary diversion.

So, why was he still thinking about Amelia? She wasn't right for him even on a temporary basis. She was uptight and upright with no imagination or sense of adventure.

Ben remembered the fire in her eyes and the way she had clung to him. He recalled the husky, sexy excitement in her voice and the soft, too-quick brush of her lips.

He thought of the uncertainty he'd seen on her face just before he left her house, and scowled. He shouldn't be thinking of her.

"Mr. Palmer," a voice called outside his door.

Ben sighed and stretched the kinks out of his shoulders. He opened the door to his service manager, Rick. "What's up?"

"There's a customer out here who insists on talking to you."

Ben sighed again and rubbed his hand through his hair. Another crabby customer. "What's the problem, Rick?"

Rick shrugged. "I dunno. It was just an oil change, but she says she needs to ask you a question."

Ben frowned. "Is she upset about something?"

Rick shook his head. "Just keeps saying she needs to see you."

One more screwy event in a screwy day. "Okay, send her in," he said, feeling his head begin to throb. Turning away, he stared out the window and considered taking a camping trip next weekend. He needed to get away from the grind. He needed to get away from his thoughts of—

"Ben?"

The voice stopped his thoughts. It was the soft, sexy voice that stroked his libido and wouldn't go away. Amelia. He turned around and glanced at her warily. She wore a long skirt and vest, discreet and feminine. His mother would approve. Hell, his grandmother would approve.

Her hair was pulled back, but a few unruly curls rebelled at the confinement. Her cheeks bloomed with color. He wondered why.

"Yes, ma'am," he drawled. "I was told you wanted to see me."

She gave a self-conscious smile. "That's right. I got an oil change for my car. Your employees have been very courteous."

"I'm glad to hear it," he said, feeling ornery enough to let her squirm a little.

She nodded, still self-conscious, and dropped her gaze from his as she meandered around his desk. "Well, I was wondering," she began and stopped when she looked up at his face.

When she lifted her fingers and gently touched his cheek, Ben stopped. Her fingers were as gentle as a butterfly's wings, and some part of her echoed the same fragility. The inborn concern and kindness he saw on her face felt like a soothing breeze. Her eyes, however, shot off glimmers of sensual curiosity.

"What happened?" she asked.

Ben wondered why his heart was racing. Must be the caffeine from the second pot of coffee he'd finished, he told himself. "Just a scrape," he said with a shrug. "I did it this morning. It's been that kind of day."

"Rough one?"

"Yeah," he said, and the devil made him add, "You wanna do something about it?"

Her eyes widened, then her gaze flittered down, and he figured he'd just scared the spit out of Miss Amelia. He watched her take a careful breath, then look up at him.

"Maybe," she said.

Ben felt a kick of surprise and arousal. She was a paradox. One minute she was shy, the next, almost bold.

"Would you like to come to my house for dinner?"

Surprised again, then wary, he shrugged. "Are you sure you won't change your mind?"

She laughed, and the sound shimmied down his nerve endings like a secret caress. "Oh, I imagine I'll change my mind a dozen times during the next hour, but dinner *will* be served at six-thirty."

What a kooky woman, he thought, but felt his curiosity teased. It was just a meal, he told himself, which meant he wouldn't have to cook or grab fast food. "Okay," he said. "Anything I can bring?"

Amelia backed away. "Just yourself." She lifted her shoulders and smiled. "And maybe your motorcycle."

Amelia was wrong. She changed her mind twenty times during the next hour. When her doorbell rang at six twenty-five, her heart jumped into her throat. There was absolutely no reason for her to lose her composure, she coached herself as she headed for the door. This was just dinner, and he was just a—

Amelia opened the door and felt her heart jump again. He was just a man, she told herself. But what a man. Looking at him, she wondered how he exuded so much— She searched her muddled mind for the correct description of exactly what he exuded, but couldn't find it. The glint in his dark gaze reflected both wickedness and amusement. She didn't know which affected her more.

"You gonna let me in?" Ben asked.

Realizing she blocked his entrance because she was gawking, Amelia felt her cheeks heat and quickly stepped aside. "Sorry. Please come in. Dinner's ready. Chicken cacciatore."

His nostrils flared slightly as he inhaled. "Smells great and I bet it tastes great, too."

"Hope so," she muttered under her breath. She was usually a decent cook, but she'd been so distracted during the meal preparation she hoped she hadn't left out any major ingredients. "Can I take your jacket?"

Ben gave her another amused glance. "You'll have to get in line. A few people have already asked for this jacket. It was worn by Evel Kneivel."

Amelia gave the worn leather jacket a closer look and shrugged in confusion. "You couldn't find a new one you liked?"

Ben chuckled. "No, Dr. Amelia. Evel Kneivel was a world-class motorcycle stunt driver. This is a collector's item. I'm a little possessive."

"Oh," Amelia said. "Sorta like Queen Victoria's jewelry on a more contemporary scale."

Ben paused, then nodded slowly. "Yeah. Something like that."

They made their way into the dining room. Ben picked up a stem of crystal and made a dinging sound with his thumb. He raised his eyebrows. "Nice stuff. You do this every night?"

Amelia tore her gaze from the way his large hand cradled the delicate goblet. "No. I haven't done it in a while."

"How come?"

She shrugged. "No guests."

She felt his searching gaze and was compelled to share more. "I was widowed last year."

He blinked. "You're kidding. You don't seem old enough to be a widow, although when I think of it, my sister lost a boyfriend when she was about your age."

"I thought it would never happen to me, but it did. So I haven't done this kind of thing in a while."

"This kind of thing?"

"Well, dinner with a man...who isn't my husband," she clarified, and immediately wished she hadn't told him. He might think she was desperate.

"How long has it been?"

"About seven years," she reluctantly revealed.

He whistled. "You must have married young."

Amelia nodded. "Right out of college. He was the boy next door. We'd known each other since elementary school, went fishing together. I can bait my own hook," she said, motioning for him to sit down and hoping to change the subject.

"Good job," he said. "I'm sure other men have asked you out since your husband died?"

Amelia nodded again and took a sip of wine. "Yes, but the timing wasn't right."

"So why me?"

Her stomach turned a flip. The way he asked was too appealing, too seductive. She thought of the reasons she'd asked him and smiled to herself. "I came across a quote the other day and it wouldn't let me go. 'If you want to feel more alive, do one thing every day that scares you.'"

She met his gaze. "You scare me."

He lifted a dark eyebrow. "Is that so? Well, tell me, Miss Amelia, what are you planning to *do* to me?"

Ten wicked possibilities instantly kicked through her mind. She tamped them all down and blew out a long sigh. "Feed you. I'm going to feed you."

He took her for a ride after dinner.

Ben liked the way her compact, feminine body wrapped around his. The way she clutched him tighter on some of the turns made him grin. When he pulled to a stop in front of her house, she looked dazed.

"You've got the bug," he said, as he helped her off the bike.

"The bug?" she repeated, lifting her bemused face upward while he removed her helmet.

"The bug for riding a motorcycle. It's in your blood now. Pretty soon you'll be driving a bike to work wearing a leather jacket embroidered Hogs Rule."

Amelia blinked as if she were trying to envision the picture. "Hogs rule," she said. "Oh, I don't think so. I imagine the college administration prefers a different image for their history professors.''

Ben shook his head and chuckled. ''Image. Whew! Must be a terrible burden to be concerned about image. I wonder if you've led a very protected life, Amelia.''

''Somewhat,'' she confessed.

''Never smoked a cigarette,'' Ben guessed.

She looked guilty. ''Well, I actually took a puff in college, but didn't like it.''

''Oh, no. How did you live with the scandal?'' he asked mockingly.

She gave him a sideways glance and walked beside him toward the front porch. ''You're poking fun.''

''Just a little. Bet you've never even gotten a speeding ticket.''

''I haven't,'' she confessed. ''But it's not because I've never gone over the speed limit.''

''Ever ditch your clothes and go swimming on a hot summer night?''

She pursed her lips slightly. ''No.''

They reached the porch, and Amelia stood with her back against the door, watching him.

He saw both curiosity and wariness in her eyes. He was surprised how much she appealed to him, and he liked the idea of disrupting her reserve, upsetting her applecart, pulling her chain.... Holding her gaze, he moved closer. ''Have you ever kissed a man who was once a bouncer?''

''Not without three beers.'' When he lowered his head to hers, her hand shot up between them. ''I've already done my scary thing today. I've met my quota.''

He grinned and moved his mouth a breath from

hers. "You might've taken care of today, but you've got a lot of yesterdays to catch up on."

"Ever trespassed before?" Ben asked Amelia the following week as he turned off the road onto a dirt trail.

Amelia tightened her arms around his waist and heard a hundred no-nos echo from her childhood. "No-o-o. Do we really *need* to trespass?"

"Yep," he said cheerfully and zoomed up a hill. He pulled to a stop and led her off the bike. "There's no better view of the valley," he said, pointing to the twinkling lights below.

"It's beautiful," she said, transfixed by the quiet beauty of the night. "Whose property—"

"Buster Granger," he said, taking her hand and leading her closer to the edge of the lookout. "He won't bother us too much if he catches us. He's got a shotgun, but can't hit the side of the barn, since he won't get his cataracts fixed."

Amelia's stomach dipped. "Why don't I feel reassured?"

Ben chuckled and slid his arm down her side. "Because I hate to tell you this, but you're a sissy."

Amelia felt a flurry of conflicting emotions. The pressure of his hand wrapped around her hip made her brain twirl like a spinning wheel. How did he make an insult sound so sexy?

"Cat got your tongue?" he asked, lowering his head closer to hers.

She took a sharp mind-clearing breath and looked at him askance. She wanted to deny his assessment, but she had no proof that she wasn't a sissy except she could put a worm on her own hook for fishing.

"If I'm such a sissy, then why did you bring me here?"

He paused and his gaze grew a shade more thoughtful. "Because it's fun. There's a lot you haven't done, and maybe I've done a little too much. When you push the limit too much, it gets boring."

She wondered at the alternating flashes of hardness and vulnerability in his eyes. She wondered why she felt both drawn to him and wary of him. "Boring, unsatisfying," she mused. "You're a paradox. One minute you give the impression of being out for a good time, then I see a glimpse of something deeper."

"Maybe," he conceded, "but don't hang your hat on it." It was a clear-cut warning. He might as well have said "Don't count on me, darlin'."

"So. I amuse you?" She wasn't sure how she felt about that possibility.

"Probably the same way I amuse you," he said, his gaze intent.

Touché, she thought and turned her gaze toward the beautiful view again.

"Tell me some more things you haven't done that you wanted to do," Ben said, squeezing her waist.

"I'm not sure that's a good idea."

"Wouldn't be prudent," he said mimicking a former president.

She sighed and tried to think of something harmless. "I've never had a kitten. My mother and my husband were allergic."

"Okay."

"I've never gone to one of those spas in New York City and gotten a makeover."

Ben snorted.

"What?" she asked, looking up at him.

"Sissy stuff."

She shouldn't be goaded. She was above this. She was too intelligent and mature to be dragged into this kind of discussion. She pulled away from him. "I've never driven a Harley."

His lips twitched. "Now, you're talking."

"*Just* talking," she told him. "That's *all.*"

"We'll see."

Three

———

"**I** don't want to go on a blind date," Amelia calmly repeated for the fifth time. She opened a reference book on the Civil War for an upcoming lecture.

"We don't always *want* to do what's best for us." Sherry paced in front of Amelia's desk. "Besides, didn't you tell me you were going to try to do one thing every day that scares you?"

Amelia regretted sharing that information with Sherry. "The prospect of a blind date doesn't scare me. It makes me nauseous."

"You're splitting hairs," Sherry said. "This is a great guy. According to my computer evaluation, he's a perfect match for your personality. Much better than that—" She stopped midstep and narrowed her eyes in a speculative glance. "You aren't still seeing Ben, are you?"

Amelia resisted the urge to squirm. "I've seen him a few times. It's nothing heavy."

Sherry sighed. "You have a crush on him, don't you?"

"No. I don't," she insisted, but her conscience was screaming. "He's just…different."

"You've got a crush on him."

"I don't."

"Then prove it. Go out with Donald Lawrence. It will serve several purposes at once. Get you out of the house, meet someone nice, help you keep your perspective about *Ben*."

Amelia pushed her hair from her face. Coming back to life was hard. The emotional coma she'd been in for the past year had felt safe, if not fulfilling. "I'll think about it."

That afternoon when she got home, she found a kitten in a box on her front porch. He was adorable and scared and feisty, and she fell in love with him on sight.

"I'm going to kill Ben," she muttered, when she got a good look at the cat's paws. Big paws. This wasn't going to be a little grown-up cat. He was going to be a big tomcat. Great, just what she needed in her life. Two tomcats.

The kitten clamped his claws around her ankle and ran her stockings. "I'm going to kill him."

Her entire evening was spent comforting the kitten. After eating, then messing on her kitchen floor, he finally settled down in her lap while she stroked him. When he began to purr, Amelia reluctantly accepted the fact that she was going to keep him. Looking at him, she decided to call him Caesar because he clearly wanted to rule the house. He fell asleep, and she gingerly placed him in a box with a warm blanket.

She put herself to bed, and just as she pulled up the covers, her phone rang. It was Ben.

"I'm going to kill you."

He gave a low chuckle that tugged at her stomach. "I figured you would. That's why I didn't drop by to see you tonight."

"A few instructions would have been nice."

"I thought the food and kitty litter would cover the bases."

"He *cried* nonstop for the first two hours."

"But you settled him down. I figured you would have a calming effect on him."

"Ben," she said as patiently as she could manage, "the prevailing wisdom on giving a pet as a surprise gift is 'don't do it.'"

"Amelia," he said in a voice that made her think of sex, "prevailing wisdom is for sissies. Night-night, sweetheart. Dream about me."

Amelia scowled. She would dream about *killing* him, she decided, as she pulled the covers over her head.

But she didn't.

She dreamed she was all alone, and it was dark and raining. Chilled to the bone, she sat under a tree with her arms wrapped tightly around her. She felt so lost and empty she was certain she had no pulse and she wasn't breathing.

She looked up, and he was standing in front of her. Ben. Her heart started to beat again. Her breath shuddered through her lungs. The sensations were both painful and exhilarating.

"I've been looking for you," he said, and pulled her into his arms.

The combined scents of his leather jacket with his clean, musky essence pervaded her mind and blood vessels. He took her mouth, and his tongue swept over hers, tasting her, coaxing her to taste him.

The rain continued to fall, drenching them. Amelia sank deeper into his kiss, clinging to his strength, absorbing his vitality.

He slid his knee between her legs, squeezing her bottom, drawing her more intimately against him. She instinctively rocked into his hardness and he moaned against her mouth.

Everything began to spin. Her clothes melted from her body like water. Ben's mouth sank to her breasts, making her cry out. He dipped his hand between her legs and found her swollen.

Amelia couldn't catch her breath, or her heart. Nothing was enough. She pulled at him, urged him, begged and pleaded. There was no shame, only need. Then he held her with his gaze and filled her. He took her and took her until he brought her all the way back to life.

Panicked, she sat straight up in bed, her heart beating a mile a minute. She put her hands to her burning cheeks. She wasn't cold. She was on fire.

Drawing in deep, ragged breaths, she closed her eyes. Breaking the silence of the night, raindrops splattered on her window. She sat for several moments, calming her mind and body.

It was only a dream, she told herself. A crazy dream.

But even when she slowly sank back down to her pillow, she still felt Ben inside her.

* * *

Ben and his nephew, Davey, were so busy throwing frosted Cheerios at each other they didn't see Maddie until she caught one of their cereal missiles.

"Food fight?" Maddie enquired with a look of motherly frustration for Ben. "This is what you're teaching him when I leave him with you on Friday nights?"

Ben groaned. "Aw, Maddie. It's not like I take him to bars or show him girlie magazines."

Maddie closed her eyes and slapped her forehead. "No, but that's coming. Right?"

Davey tossed another Cheerio that hit Maddie's chin. "Mo-om, don't you like Cheerios?"

Maddie's lips twitched, and she quickly moved closer to give Davey a hug. "Yes, I do. But I like to *eat* them."

Davey gave a little-boy shrug. "Ben says throwing food is a guy thing."

"Hmm. We'll see. Thanks for taking care of my gorgeous, terrific son." Maddie gave Ben a sideways glance at the same time she picked up Davey. "Brother mine, when are you going to get serious with a woman so you can have food fights with your very own miniature human replica?"

Ben snorted. "Get serious with a woman? Never."

Maddie sighed. "I'm not joking. You're missing out on something that could make you very happy. Underneath that rebel-without-a-pause exterior you're a great guy."

Ben deliberately hooked his foot over the edge of the table and leaned back in his chair. "Why is it that married people can't be happy unless they're converting single people into wedded bliss?"

Maddie ignored his question. "Are you seeing anyone now?"

Ben shrugged, thinking of Amelia. "Yeah, but it's just for fun. Nothing heavy. She's not my type."

"Why?" Maddie asked in a dry voice. "Does she prefer a Kawasaki over a Harley?"

He chuckled. "She probably wouldn't know the difference."

Maddie's eyes widened. "She's not a Hog rider? Oh, my goodness. But does she have a tattoo?"

Uncomfortable with his sister's curiosity, he dropped his foot to the floor and rose from the table. "I can't be sure, but I would guess not."

"Be still my beating heart. Don't toy with me, Ben. You're not *really* going out with a *nice* girl, are you?"

Ben sighed. "She's nice. She's not my type, and I'm not hers. We—" He hesitated because he felt a niggling of discomfort. He shook it off. "We amuse each other. That's all."

Ben rounded the corner to Amelia's street and spotted an unfamiliar sedan pulling into Amelia's driveway behind her car. Easing down on the throttle, he pulled to a stop and watched.

In the glow of her floodlight, Ben saw a man get out of the car and open the door for her, then walk her to the porch.

Amelia had a date?

A mixture of amusement and irritation thudded through him. No big deal, he told himself. There were no strings between them. She amused him. She was sweet, and something about her made him feel protective of her, but she would never keep him awake nights.

Still uncomfortable, he narrowed his eyes.

Ben watched the guy dip his head as if he were going to kiss her. His gut tightened, and some unnamed primitive instinct coursed through his blood. His hands clenched his bike grips.

Amelia moved away and shook her head.

Ben's body relaxed. Slightly. His gut was still tense. He didn't like this. He didn't like it at all. He sucked in a deep breath of air and rode out of the neighborhood. The roar of the engine would clear his mind.

He meandered through backroads for thirty minutes, assuring himself his feelings had been a momentary aberration. The familiar sensation of cold wind on his face blew his crazy thoughts out of his head. He could have easily gone home, but amused curiosity lured him back to her house.

When Amelia answered the door, he leaned against the doorjamb and cracked a smile. "So, why didn't you kiss him?"

She blinked her eyes in surprise, then her cheeks bloomed with color and she straightened. "I didn't want to kiss him."

"You kissed me," he said, the devil nudging him to get under her skin.

She lifted her chin, and Ben was halfway sure she would sprout the word *prim* on her forehead. "You were more forceful."

He raised his eyebrows. "Oh, I *forced* you?"

Amelia sighed and opened the door. "Would you like to come in?"

"I'd love to. Did you let Mr. Mercedes in? If you

see him again, tell him he might need to get his carburetor checked. It was noisy.''

''I'll remember that,'' she said, walking toward her den and sitting in a chair.

''You didn't answer my question,'' Ben said. ''Did you invite Mr. Mercedes in?''

''I didn't,'' she said, then met his gaze. ''Why do you ask?''

Ben felt the searching power of her blue eyes and had to fight his own urge to squirm. ''I'm curious.''

She nodded. ''He was a blind date. My friend, Sherry, did some kind of computer romance chart and decided I should go out with him.''

Ben cocked his head to one side and shook his head. ''Well, I'll be damned. A computer romance chart. What'd you think of him?''

''He was well educated, conscientious, kind, well mannered—''

''Bored the hell out of you, huh?'' he asked, propping himself on the side of the overstuffed chair where she sat.

Her lips twitched. ''I hadn't planned on saying that.''

''But since I did...'' he said with a grin.

Amelia sighed. Ben was the most disruptive, disturbing man she'd ever met. ''Since you did, I'll have to agree. He didn't hold my attention.''

''Wonder why?''

''I guess he didn't *scare* me enough,'' she said, then stood.

Ben snagged her wrist and pulled her back to him, drawing her between his knees. ''So tell me, Miss Amelia, why'd you let me kiss you?''

He pulled her still closer. Her breasts brushed

against his chest, and her nipples tightened. She felt annoyed. She felt aroused. The combination was potent, making her bold. "Has anyone ever told you that you're incredibly cocky?" she asked, sliding her arms around his neck.

His mouth quirked in a sexy half grin. "They don't usually put it that nicely, but I'm not usually in the company of such a nice girl."

Nice girl. Amelia felt a decidedly not-nice rush of heat. For the past twenty-eight years, being a nice girl had been fine with Amelia. Why did the description suddenly bother her?

Ben must have seen the shift inside her. His gaze deepened, and with his hand against the small of her back, he pressed her intimately against his masculinity.

Amelia's heart hammered against her rib cage. He'd made a blatantly sexual move. At another time she would have pulled away. With another man she would have pulled away.

But his gaze still held hers, and her body moved instinctively, undulating against his hardness.

Ben sucked in a quick, sharp breath and he slid a hand up her rib cage to cup her breast through the thin fabric of her blouse. "Are you asking for trouble?"

He rubbed his thumb over her taut nipple, and she closed her eyes. "I don't know," she managed, lifting her mouth to his. "Am I?"

He took her lips, plundering her recesses with his tongue. She felt gloriously consumed. Spinning out of control, Amelia held tightly to his strong shoulders and matched his sensuality with her curiosity.

Ben shuddered and lowered his lips to a breast,

taking her nipple into his mouth though the blouse. He squeezed her bottom and urged her against him.

She moaned, growing swollen. She wanted more of him. Less between them.

Ben pulled back and swore. He stared at her with eyes darkened by passion. "Don't push me, Amelia. What do you want?"

Shivering, she searched for the words, the thoughts, the feelings. "I want," she began, her voice cracking. Overwhelmed by her emotions, she swallowed. "I want you to make me feel alive."

He drew in a long breath and stared at her. "I'm no Prince Charming."

She shook her head. "And I'm not Sleeping Beauty."

He laughed without humor. "But you could be," he said, easing her away from him.

She had to swallow a protest and clasp her hands together to keep from reaching for him. It had felt so right to be in his arms.

"I'll never be a prince, Amelia. You need to understand that. Happily ever after is not gonna happen with me."

Four

It surprised the hell out of Ben when he spotted Amelia at the preseason basketball game between Salem College and Randolph Macon. She wore one of her feminine dresses with a hem that hit just below her knees, flat shoes and her untamable hair pulled back from her face.

It was too easy to remember how she'd felt pressed against him. Too easy to remember how he'd wanted to take her right there in the overstuffed chair in her living room. But he knew she was off-limits. That was why he hadn't called her or gone to see her.

He told himself he could look away, but he watched her instead. Her wide eyes followed the action of the game. There was a sweetness combined with a hidden fire in Amelia that drew him. He felt a strange tug in his gut at the sight of her standing on the sidelines.

He figured he would avoid her just as he had for the past two weeks, but fate turned her gaze toward his. She stared at him for a moment, then deliberately looked away. In that moment Ben felt both a sting of irritation and a kick of amusement. He'd just been snubbed.

Ben supposed the socially correct behavior would be for them to mutually ignore each other. In his twenty-nine years on the planet, however, he'd rarely chosen socially correct behavior. He moved from his seat on the bleachers toward her.

"I didn't know you were a basketball fan," he said to her.

Amelia kept her gaze glued to the game. "I'm not. I have a student with a basketball scholarship who needed some extra help. We negotiated that he would do a second rewrite on a paper if I came to this game."

"Do one thing every day that scares you?" Ben said.

"Watching isn't scary. Playing would be scary."

The buzzer sounded for halftime and Amelia waved to one of the players. The same player waved to both Ben and Amelia.

"That's Jerry," Ben said. "He's one of my kids."

Amelia swerved her head to look at him. "*Your* kids?"

Ben shrugged. "Yeah. I play basketball every week with some kids with the Youth League downtown. He's one of our success stories."

"He's the one who had to do the rewrite." Confusion wrinkled her brow. "And you played basketball with him?"

"Yep, and warned him against the woes of making

bad choices. Youth League's way of trying to keep kids out of trouble.''

She was silent for a moment, confusion still marring her face. ''But haven't you been in trouble with the law?''

He wondered how she knew that. ''Yep, but mostly misdemeanors. The organizer of the group told me I'm the example of how a bad boy can turn out okay.''

Amelia nodded slowly as if she weren't totally convinced. She glanced away. ''Well, enjoy the game,'' she said in a dismissive voice and started to leave.

Surprised, Ben stepped in front of her. ''No need to rush off. Where are your manners, Miss Amelia?''

Her eyes widened, and Ben wondered if he should duck from the shooting sparks. ''*My* manners.'' She inhaled quickly and lifted her chin. ''I believe you owe me an apology. However,'' she said, holding up her hand when he would have interrupted. ''You're probably unfamiliar with the words *I'm sorry.*''

''An apology,'' Ben said, confounded. ''Why in hell do I owe you an apology?''

She glanced on either side of them, but seemed to overcome her discomfort for arguing in public. ''You made an assumption. Have you heard the cute little play on the word *assume?* When you assume, you make an ass out of 'u' and 'me.'''

Ben squelched the impulse to point out how sexy and cute she looked when she was angry. ''Can't say I've heard it before. So what did I assume?''

''You assumed that I would *want* happily ever after with you. Well, I'll tell you something, Mr.—'' She shook her head as if she were so frustrated she couldn't recall his name.

Underneath the anger, Ben saw a sliver of hurt in her eyes that squeezed his heart. He tried to help her out. "Mr. Palmer."

"Mr. Super Stud," she corrected. "I've had happily ever after, and it didn't turn out happy. So I'm not looking for happily ever after with *any* man right now. Especially you."

She turned on her heel, and Ben felt the slight breeze of her abrupt departure while he tried to get past the fact that she'd called him Super Stud. Instinct made his feet move after her. He caught up with her just as she left the gym.

"Now hold on," he began.

"I'm not talking with you. You've insulted me. You owe me an apology and I *know* you're not the kind of man to ever admit you're wrong."

"Amelia," he said, his own temper kicking in. "You took it the wrong way. I—"

"No, I didn't," she insisted, moving down the hall. "And I'm not going to talk with you."

"Yes, you will," he said, stepping in front of her.

"No, I won't. I'm going to a place where even you can't go," she told him as she walked around him.

"Where—"

"The ladies' room," she said, and let the door swing in his face.

Ben rested his arms on his hips and took a deep breath. Their conversation stuck in his craw. Their relationship, if such a thing existed, stuck in his craw. She wasn't the usual kind of woman he dated. She was too ladylike, too vulnerable, too emotional.

He hated the idea of hurting her. That was why he'd warned her off the other night. It had nothing to do with any confusing feelings he might have for her.

Ben swore. He hated to admit it, but she was right about a few things. She was, however, wrong about a few, and he would set her straight on those. The first was whether or not he would go into a ladies' room.

He pushed open the door and called out. "Man in the room."

There was only one other woman besides Amelia in the large bathroom, and she quickly left.

Amelia, standing in front of the mirror, gaped at him. "Have you lost your mind? You're not supposed to be in here. This is the ladies' room."

He gave a wry chuckle. "It's not my first time."

Her eyes widened, then she closed them. "Oh, I don't want to hear this."

"Sure you do. Listen carefully. I'm sorry I acted like an ass."

Her eyes popped open. "Pardon?"

Ben gave a put-upon sigh. "Just like a woman. Once is not enough. You gotta repeat it. Last time," he warned. "I'm sorry I acted like an ass."

She looked bewildered and beautiful and lost for words. "We need to get out of here," she finally murmured, and led the way out of the room.

As he left, Ben held the door open for a confused-looking woman. "Anytime," he said after she thanked him.

Amelia groaned and shook her head.

Ben stepped beside her. "Now you have to keep your end of the bargain."

Amelia gaped at him. "What is *my* end of the bargain?"

He shrugged. "You have to talk to me."

She hesitated an unflattering extra few seconds, then nodded. "Okay."

Ben followed instincts that were likely to lead him straight to hell, but he wanted under her skin. "Ride with me to get ice cream at the Salem Ice Cream Parlor."

Amelia shook her head. "I'm not dressed—"

"For kidnapping?" he asked, feeling the devil rise within him again. He wondered how such a sweet female could provoke him in so many ways. Damned if he wasn't going to find out.

She gave him a warning glance. "For riding."

"Sissy excuse."

"It's November. It's too cold for ice cream."

"More sissy excuses."

"I promised Jerry I would watch the game."

Her wary glance slid away, but Ben had no intention of letting her retreat. "Okay. We'll go afterward."

"What do you want?" Ben asked.

She still couldn't believe he'd apologized. As she looked around the ice cream parlor decorated with bits of nostalgia, Amelia's teeth continued to chatter. She clamped her jaw together and shivered. "I want a cup of hot chocolate and a hot bath."

Ben chuckled as he looked her up and down. "That dress is pretty, but it's too thin. Here." He rubbed his hands over her arms to warm her.

"I told you I wasn't dressed for riding."

"Hey, Ben, you assaulting my customers?" the guy behind the counter asked.

"No. You should thank me. I'm using my influence to bring you new customers."

"Influence," Amelia echoed in a dark voice.

What kind of insanity held her in its grip when Ben was around? Why had she agreed to freeze herself half to death to join him for ice cream? Every time she thought she'd figured him out, he did something to broaden her view of him. Every time she talked herself into dismissing him, he did something different that snagged her interest again.

She'd decided he was egotistical and callous, then he apologized. She'd thought him careless, yet, even now, he was trying to warm her. Amelia's heart bumped into a faster rhythm.

He covered her cold nose with his fingers. "Okay. I've tortured you. Let me make it up to you. What do you want?"

"Something hot. Something very hot."

He gave her a sexy grin and quickly pressed his mouth against hers. "Now 'hot' is something I can arrange."

"Ben!" a woman's voice called out in surprise and pleasure.

Ben immediately pulled back and groaned. "Maddie," he said. "What are you doing here?"

An attractive red-haired woman with curious brown eyes bounced up to them. "I was on my way home from the mall and decided to pick up some ice cream for Davey and Joshua." She smiled, giving Amelia an inquisitive gaze. "Introduce me," she commanded Ben.

Ben sighed. "Amelia, this is my sister, Maddie."

"It's nice to meet you," Amelia said.

"And it's so nice to meet you." Maddie pumped Amelia's hand. "I don't usually get to meet Ben's gir—"

Ben cleared his throat loudly and gave Maddie an ominous look.

"Friends," Maddie corrected. "He's so busy. I don't usually get to meet his friends. How long have you known each other?"

Amelia glanced at Ben who looked like he wanted to jump out of his skin. "Not long. Ben is teaching me to ride a motorcycle. It's something I've always wanted to do."

Maddie glanced at Amelia's dress and nodded slowly. "Really?"

"Well, not today," Amelia told her. "We just ran into each other at the Salem College basketball game today. I teach history there."

Maddie's eyes widened. "You teach history," she squeaked and looked at Ben for an explanation.

Amelia sensed that Ben didn't like explaining relationships to his sister. "Yes. Did you attend Salem College?"

Maddie shook her head. "Oh, no. I went to travel school. I always wanted to take a few college courses. Maybe I will." She glanced at her watch. "Listen, I don't need to get home quite yet. I'd love to sit with you two for a few minutes. You don't mind," she added meaningfully to Ben, "do you?"

Ben made a strangled sound, and Amelia found both their gazes pinning her to the wall. Feeling incredibly awkward, she shrugged and looked toward Ben. "I don't mind if—"

"That settles it," Maddie said cheerfully.

For the next thirty minutes, Maddie quizzed Amelia in a friendly way. She sympathized with the loss of Amelia's husband and expressed admiration for her career. Then she regaled them with stories of Ben's childhood. Ben looked as if he were being subjected to Chinese water torture. By the time Maddie finished, Amelia had gotten an earful.

"The Bad Boys Club," Amelia said to Ben after Maddie left.

"It was an exclusive club," he told her. "Membership was limited."

Amelia chuckled. "I'm sure it was. I shudder to think what the initiation was."

"It wasn't that bad. We all wanted tattoos."

Amelia rolled her eyes. "I imagine your mothers were delighted with the idea of you permanently defacing your skin."

Ben stared at her for a long moment, saying nothing.

Amelia got an uneasy feeling. She lowered her voice. "You didn't really get a tattoo."

"Not while I was in the Bad Boys Club. Later."

She swallowed a gasp. "But I haven't seen it. What is it? What in the world possessed you to—"

Ben covered her mouth. "You haven't seen it because my clothes cover it most of the time."

Her eyes widened. "You have a tattoo on your—" she dipped her head and whispered "—butt!"

Ben chuckled. "No. On my arm. It's a snake."

She looked at him as if he'd sprouted an extra head. Although he wouldn't admit it under penalty of death, Ben had yearned for the ability to erase the tattoo more than a few times. He leaned forward and toyed with her bottom lip with his thumb. "Wanna see my tattoo?" he asked with a grin.

Amelia tried, unsuccessfully, to purse her lips. "It's not nece—"

"Sissy," Ben said, still playing with her lip.

Her eyes darkened, and she clamped her perfect white teeth over his thumb.

Ben stared at her in surprise. "You bit me."

Horrified, Amelia pulled back and covered her mouth. Her face blazed with color. "I'm so sorry. I can't believe I did that." She reached for his thumb and shook her head. "I don't know what came over me. I've never bitten anyone in my life. Even when I was a child…"

She was so appalled at herself that Ben took pity on her. "It's not that big of a deal."

"Yes, it is. You don't understand. I have *never* done that before! It's *you!*" she said, raising her voice. "You are making me crazy. You're making me—" She looked as if she were searching for the words.

Ben felt compassion for her, but he also had to nearly choke himself to keep from laughing.

She glared at him and stood. "You're making me *do things. Crazy things.* It's *you!*"

"Oh, no," he said, standing, too. "You're not putting that on me. I didn't tell you to bite me."

"You might as well have, when you called me a sissy," she retorted, then cringed. "Good Lord, where did that come from?"

"Chill out, Miss Amelia," Ben said. "It was just a little nip. I've had a lot worse."

"Now, we're going to discuss your sexual history?" she said in a high-pitched voice, then shook her head. "I need some air," she told him, and turned toward the door.

Ben strode after her, joining her outside. "You're overreacting."

"I don't think so. I've never—"

Ben caught her arm and turned her around. "Well, maybe you should have."

She went silent, staring into his gaze as if she were drinking him from a cup. The look in her eyes went straight to his gut.

He pulled her against him. "Maybe you should have bitten someone. And if it'll make you feel any better, Amelia," he said, surprised at the huskiness he heard in his own voice, "you can bite me anytime you want."

Amelia wasn't exactly sure what it was, but something had come over her since she'd met Ben, and it wasn't all bad. She was starting to look at things in a different way. She was starting to see herself in a different way. After all those years of trying to please Charles, now the only person she truly needed to please was herself.

It was both a liberating and challenging realization. Challenging because she wasn't always sure what she wanted.

She experimented with new recipes, bought new CDs, checked out different clothing styles and thought about cutting her hair.

One day, a lingerie mail-order catalog that had been passed around the office landed on her desk. Normally she would have passed it on without a glance. Instead she flipped it open.

Sherry burst into her office. "I've got another blue-chip bachelor for you. He's not as—" She stopped, eyeing the lingerie catalog. "Omigoodness. Will wonders never cease. Amelia has progressed to bad-girl underwear?"

Amelia refused to blush. "I was just looking."

"You're doing a lot of that lately, aren't you?"

"Yes. Figuring out what I like and what I don't like." She smiled. "It's strange to be doing this at twenty-eight. I realized I haven't made any decisions that weren't heavily influenced by Charles."

"And how does Ben Palmer figure into all this?"

Amelia sighed. "He makes me crazy."

"Good crazy or bad crazy?"

"Both, but you don't need to worry," she assured Sherry. "I know he's temporary. I know he won't be around long. We've laid the ground rules."

"And they are?"

"We amuse each other, and neither of us is interested in happily ever after." She changed the subject by pointing to a picture in the catalog. "Aren't those corset-looking bras uncomfortable?"

"The ones that look like they hike your breasts up to your chin?" Sherry asked wryly. "The man who designed them might have the aerodynamics down, but I think surgery would be less painful. If you want to ease into this stuff, you might start with the thong panties."

"In November?" Amelia made a face. "Isn't that a little breezy?"

Sherry closed the catalog. "Amelia, are you going to get burned by Ben?"

Amelia took a deep breath and resolutely shook her head. "I'm not going to get burned, because I don't have unrealistic expectations. He's very different, not that I have a wide range of experience. But I know I'm definitely out of my league."

Sherry arched her eyebrows. "Yeah, well he's definitely out of his league, too."

* * *

"Glad you could come, Ben," Jenna Jean Michaels said with a smile. "It does my heart good to see you on the right side of the law."

"I'll do just about anything to get into your cookies," Ben told her. "Even volunteer to be Santa for the Youth League Christmas party."

"Hey, nobody gets into my wife's cookies except me," Stan Michaels said in a mock-gangster voice. "I wouldn't want to have to hurt you."

"You and what army, Stan my man," Ben jeered, reminding Stan of his Bad Boys Club nickname.

"No spitting," Jenna warned. "If you're going to do that stupid Bad Boys Club handshake with the spitting, then take it outside."

Ben blew her a kiss, then took a bite of cookie.

Ben had known Jenna Jean and her rascally husband, Stanley Michaels, almost as long as he'd been on this earth. Jenna Jean had grown up to be Roanoke's assistant commonwealth attorney and Stanley was a doctor. Heavily involved with the Youth League, the two were holding a casual cocktail party to drum up support for upcoming events.

Jenna Jean pushed a beer into Ben's hand. "I talked to Maddie two days ago. She says your new girlfriend is very different. Education is way past eighth grade. No prior criminal record. And no visible tattoos."

Immediately on guard, Ben washed the bite of cookie down with the beer. "She's not a girlfriend. She's just a friend."

"Uh-huh," Jenna said in complete disbelief. "If she's not a girlfriend, then why were you kissing her in the Salem Ice Cream Parlor?"

Stan whistled. "Sounds like an interrogation to me."

"She's not a girlfriend," Ben insisted. "She's not my type."

"Not your type might be a very good thing," Jenna said cheerfully.

"She's too nice," Ben muttered. "Surprised the hell out of me when she bit me."

"She bit you!" Stan said, and roared with laughter. "Well, there's definitely hope. Remember how Jenna Jean bit me when we were kids. She even left a scar."

Jenna gave a heavy sigh, then kissed her husband on the cheek. "You never quit with that story. I need to mingle," she told them and glanced at Ben. "I'd like to meet her."

"Is that a royal command?" Ben asked.

"Always," she said in a playfully snooty voice. "Seriously, Ben," she added, "if she's not your type, that's probably a good thing."

It might be a good thing, but Ben had already decided he and Amelia were not going to be lovers, no matter how tempted he might be.

Five

Amelia didn't notice the date until she was halfway through the day. She had an odd sense that something was missing, but pushed it aside. Heaven knows, she'd had that feeling more often than not. It was a Saturday, so she'd slept in a little and splurged on a manicure. It wouldn't make the front-page news, but Amelia's fingernails were now painted winterberry. She kept looking at them and smiling.

Afterward she ran errands, picked up dry cleaning and went to the grocery store. All through the morning and afternoon, she felt something vague nudging her under her skin. Funny, it didn't hit her until she was shopping for fruit. She automatically skipped the oranges because Charles preferred bananas and apples. When she checked for bruises on a golden delicious apple, she realized today was Charles's birthday.

Amelia's heart squeezed tight. Had she really almost forgotten? Distress crowded her chest. What did that say about her? She didn't want to forget Charles. He'd been an important part of her life, an encompassing part of her life.

She hurried through her shopping and rushed home. Once she put everything away, she didn't know what to do with herself. She didn't want to call her mother and reminisce. She didn't want to call a new friend who hadn't known Charles. She didn't want to stay home.

At a loss, she grabbed an old photo album and headed for the park. Charles had always enjoyed the park.

Five minutes away from giving up on her, Ben sat on his bike and watched Amelia pull into her driveway. They'd made casual plans to get together tonight, but hadn't nailed down a time.

She got out of her car and quickly headed for her front door.

"Hey, Miss Amelia," Ben called.

Swinging around, she stared at him. "Ben! I didn't see you."

He walked toward her. "I got that impression. I was starting to wonder if I was being stood up."

Her eyes widened. "I forgot. I'm so sorry. I completely forgot. I've been very distracted today." She crammed her key in the lock and led the way into her house. "Weird day," she murmured.

"Weird," he echoed, trying to read her. Something wasn't right. Her hair in beguiling disarray, she was dressed casually in jeans and a pea coat. She looked fidgety and unsettled. She played with the edge of the big book she carried.

"What's that?" he asked, moving closer.

"Oh." She glanced down and shrugged. "It's just an album. What can I get you to drink?"

He snagged her arm before she could leave. "What's up?"

"Nothing," she said, but her eyes glinted with unshed tears.

"Where did you go today?" he continued, feeling a strange protectiveness toward her.

"To get a manicure and to the grocery store," she said in an unsteady voice. She took a deep breath, and the pain in her eyes deepened. "I went to the park. You see, this was Charles's birthday, and I didn't know what to do." Clearly distraught, she pushed her hair behind her ear. "I mean, I haven't read any articles about what to do on your former husband's birthday. I almost forgot it, and I felt so guilty—"

The phone rang, and Amelia cringed. "Oh, no. That's probably my mother."

"Want me to get it?"

She made a sound that sounded almost like a laugh. "No, I'd better take it."

With a mixture of odd feelings, Ben took Amelia's album and sat down in a chair while she chatted with her mother. Thumbing through the photo album, he listened to Amelia talk about Charles and their life together. The pictures showed all the "firsts" they'd shared. In the sprinkler, walking to school, roller skating. He told himself he couldn't be envious of a dead man, but Ben felt a damn strange longing when he saw the pictures of Amelia as a child and a teenager.

He couldn't explain it, but he wished he had known her then.

He wished he had known her when her two front teeth were missing, and later when she wore braces. In all the photos of her, from the time she was a young child until now, he saw the same gentle, sunshiny spark in her eyes.

He couldn't help noticing how the pictures of Charles reflected a man who grew increasingly conservative as the years passed. Much of Amelia's outer appearance reflected that conservative bent, except for the spark in her eyes. Out of nowhere the thought entered his head that perhaps Charles might not have been the best man for Amelia.

Swallowing an oath at his twisted musing, he closed the album. It didn't matter what Ben thought. The fact remained that Charles had been Amelia's husband, and Charles was dead.

She twirled the telephone cord and gave a sad smile.

"Yes, Mom, I remember the first time I saw snow was when I went to Sugar Mountain with his family. He taught me how to sled and ski. We got into a snowball fight and I ended up with a black eye."

In one way he felt as if he were violating her privacy. In another way, though, he sensed she wanted him to stay.

Amelia hung up the phone and moved next to his chair. "Sorry. Let's see. Where were we? I was getting you something to drink."

The faraway look in her gaze grabbed and twisted something inside him. Ben tugged her into his lap. "No. You were telling me about your visit to the park."

She closed her eyes. "You don't really want me to do that because then I might cry and I bet you hate it when women cry."

Ben would normally be the first to run for the door when a woman started crying, but heaven help him, she reminded him of a lost child. He pulled her into his arms and hugged her.

She wept. For several moments, she cried on his shoulder, dampening his jacket with her tears. When she finally lifted her head, she tugged a lady's handkerchief from her pocket and delicately blew her nose.

"It's not that I miss him so much," she said, then looked stricken. "That sounded horrible, didn't it?"

Ben wryly shook his head. "You're gonna have to work a lot harder to sound horrible."

She sighed. "Part of me feels guilty about going on with my life, but I don't want to live the rest of my life in mourning. I want to have another snowball fight. I want to ride a motorcycle. I want to eat oranges."

"Oranges?" Ben echoed.

"He never liked them, but I do. I want to have a life. I want to live."

"There's nothing wrong with that."

"Then why does it feel wrong?"

"There's probably a deep psychological reason like you feel guilty that he died in the accident and you didn't." Ben sensed Amelia was desperately looking for a ray of light. His natural irreverence surfaced. "Or it might just be that you're a sissy."

She dipped her head and gave a breathy laugh. "I think you got a little more than you bargained for tonight. Weepy female."

Ben pushed a strand of hair from her face. "I didn't do too bad. I've got a beautiful woman in my lap."

She lifted her gaze to meet his, then lifted her fingers to his jaw. "You've been awfully kind for someone with a snake tattoo."

Ben squelched a ripple of awareness. Her body felt soft and warm against his, her bottom enticingly snug between his legs. Knowing she was vulnerable right now, he struggled with his desire.

"You want to see my tattoo now?" he asked, shrugging out of his jacket. He pushed the sleeve of his white Henley up his arm, baring his biceps.

"It's a cobra," she said, "with fangs." Her lips twitched as she looked at him. "What possessed you to do this?"

"A bottle of tequila in Cozumel, Mexico. The last thing I remember was a line dance in Carlos 'n' Charlie's bar. The next morning I woke up on the beach with a cobra on my arm."

She ran her fingers over his biceps. "I have to say this is the first time I've been up close and personal with a tattoo."

"It's a tough job, but somebody's gotta do it," he said, then felt a strange twinge. "I wish I'd been the one to give you a black eye with your first snowball battle."

Still stroking his skin, she gave him a sideways glance. "I'm not sure how to take that."

"I would've liked to have known you when you were a kid," Ben said, sifting his fingers through her hair again.

"But I was a sissy."

He shook his head. "Nah. Sissiness is a learned

behavior. I looked at some of your pictures. You were a hellion in hiding.''

She slid her hand under the edge of his sleeve and glanced up at him, her expression shielded by her eyelashes. ''And what am I now?''

Ben's heart thumped at the subtle invasion of her fingers on his shoulder. ''You're coming out of hiding.''

She slowly met his gaze, and Ben felt the impact of her expression like a bold caress. She wanted him. She probably had no clue what she would be getting herself into, but she wanted him. The knowledge rippled through him, making him hard. She was unlike any other woman he'd known. She was so very tender, yet underneath it all there was a wildness.

Determined not to seduce her, he narrowed his eyes and waited for the moment to pass. It would pass. She would back down. She would come to her senses.

Instead, moving inch by mesmerizing inch, Amelia lifted her mouth to his and whispered, ''Thank you.'' Then she kissed him.

Sliding her delicate fingers through his hair to his scalp, she gently guided his lips against hers. She opened her mouth, sucking on his bottom lip, then slid her tongue over his.

It was too sexy, too erotic to resist. Ben wondered how a woman could do too little and too much at the same time. Even through her blouse and his shirt, he could feel the hardened tips of her breasts against his chest. He wondered if she knew how aroused he was. With the instinct of a temptress, she undulated her bottom against him.

Ben groaned. He wondered how long he could play

with her and still not take her. He wondered how far he could go without going too far.

She rubbed her open mouth back and forth against his lips, and Ben started to sweat.

"You feel hot," she murmured.

"I am," he said, tugging her blouse free from her jeans.

"I am, too," she whispered, and pulled his shirt loose. She immediately slid her hands up his chest.

He immediately slid his hands over her breasts. She gave a soft little gasp and pushed herself against him. Everything about her, every movement she made, every breath she took was begging for more.

Ben buried his face in her neck, inhaling her sweet, seductive scent as he played with her nipple. With his other hand he unfastened her jeans and eased his fingers past the lace barrier. He waited to see if she wanted him to stop.

Instead, she urged his mouth back to hers and took his lips in a mind-blowing kiss. His pulse thudded through all his pleasure points. He wanted her naked lying across his naked body. He wanted to see her hair skim across his chest and belly as she kissed him intimately. He wanted to feel her wet and swollen for him. He wanted to be inside her.

He slid his hand between her thighs and found her wet and wanting. The knowledge, the sensation, pushed him on. He stroked the silken bead of her femininity. She moaned, and the sound was so sexual, Ben knew he would pay for even that small pleasure.

He plunged his finger inside her, and she cried out, shattering around him. She trembled in his arms, pressing her mouth to his with breathless, sensual kisses. When she reached for his zipper, Ben stayed her hand.

"Why?" she asked, her eyes still unbearably dark with passion.

"It's not the right time," he managed, some foreign need to DO THE RIGHT THING screaming at him to stop. His mind was clouded with passion, but a deep instinct demanded he stop. He'd never experienced it before, so it confused the hell out of him.

"It's fair," she said, sliding his zipper down. The slow whisking sound was one more unbearable temptation. If she touched him, if she let him inside... "You made me—"

Ben gulped in a deep breath of air and shook his head. "This isn't about fair. It's just—"

"Just what?"

"Just crazy," he said, his brain and body throbbing with need.

"I want to touch you," she told him. "I want to—"

He covered her mouth. "You don't know what you want right now. You're still missing your husband. We've made enough confusion for one night. We don't need any more." For a moment he thought he'd offended her and she would tell him to leave. Part of him wished she would. She surprised him again, however, and flung her arms around him.

Wary and fascinated, Ben stared down at the woman in his arms. Surely a nice little widow history professor couldn't get under his skin.

"You'll take your first lesson here," Ben said, pulling his Harley onto a dirt track. "Riding one of those." He pointed to several minibikes padlocked in a cage. "I know the owner, and he gave me the key for the evening."

The butterflies in Amelia's stomach immediately stopped dancing. "This doesn't scare me," she said, referring to her personal challenge to do one thing every day that scared her.

Ben chuckled and helped her off his bike. "You have to crawl before you walk."

She lifted the visor on her helmet and studied him. "Did you?"

"That's different."

"Uh-huh," she said. "Is this a chromosome theory?"

"No, this is based on talent and expertise."

"And you came out of the womb with an Easy Rider sign flashing on your forehead?"

"No, but I was always the best bike rider in the neighborhood."

"Oh," Amelia said, remembering she'd had the distinction of using training wheels the longest. Deciding not to share that fact with Ben, she headed for the minibikes.

"Go ahead and sit on it," he told her, then gave her instructions for starting, accelerating and braking. "Don't go too fast."

"It sounds like a lawn mower," she yelled at him after starting the engine. "When do I get to ride a *real* motorcycle?"

"When I say so," he yelled back.

Amelia stuck her tongue out at him and buzzed away. She heard him yell something else after her that sounded like "too fast," but decided not to watch the speedometer. Despite her initial disappointment, she enjoyed zipping around the track and pushing the meager limits of the minibike.

She spotted a trail leading off from the track and, giving a quick wave to Ben, took off to explore. Minutes later Ben hunted her down and pointed her back to the track. Daylight was waning, and Ben was none too happy with her.

"You've done enough for one day," he told her, after he returned the minibike to a cage. "Are you sure you've never gotten a speeding ticket? Didn't you hear me tell you to slow down and stay on the track?"

"I've never gotten a speeding ticket. I just wanted to see how fast a little bike like that would go."

He took her shoulders in his hands and looked into her eyes, as serious as she'd ever seen him. "I don't want you to get hurt."

Her heart turned over. "I don't want to get hurt, either, but we both know there are no guarantees."

He didn't like her response. He didn't say it, but she could read it on his face.

There was much, however, that Amelia couldn't read about Ben, she thought as they rode home. Since that night he'd stopped their lovemaking, she'd sensed more reticence than ever from him. It was strange, but she trusted him more now. She wanted to be closer to him, yet he seemed to hold her at arm's length.

When he walked her to her front porch and kissed her, it was so easy to sink into his arms. He made it too easy to want him to the point of distraction. When he pulled away, she sighed. "Would you like to come in?"

"I better not," he murmured, and kissed her again.

"Why not?" she asked, sliding her hands under his jacket to the warmth of his chest.

Ben groaned.

"I only bite on request."

He swore softly, then set her away from him. "You go inside," he told her.

Amelia felt a sliver of doubt. Perhaps the wanting was more one-sided than she'd thought. Her upbringing kept her from being too bold.

"Be a good girl and go inside," Ben said with a half grin.

Unsettled, Amelia frowned. "Thank you for the lesson," she muttered, and pushed open her door.

"Think you'll stop by the sale tomorrow?" Ben asked. "It'll be like a carnival."

"Probably."

He nodded. "'Night, Amelia."

Feeling very confused, she watched him leave as the cat wove around her ankles. Ben didn't make sense. One minute he was pushing her away. The next he was making sure he would see her again. He could have had her last week, but he hadn't taken her even though he'd wanted her. Maybe he hadn't wanted her that much. Maybe she didn't "reboot his hard drive" as Sherry would put it.

Something else chafed at her, too. *Be a good girl.* Amelia shut the door and absently picked up the cat. For the first time in her life, she wondered what it would be like if she weren't quite so "good."

Ben's sister, Maddie, balanced a boy on her knee and pink cotton candy in her hand as she waved to Amelia. "Come on over," she called.

Amelia looked around the busy foreign car lot in

amazement. A band played rock 'n' roll oldies while people swayed to the music. She spotted others getting their picture taken in a vintage convertible Jaguar. The scent of hot dogs and cotton candy filled the air. "Ben said it was like a carnival, but I didn't expect this."

Maddie nodded. "The previous owner started this tradition, and Ben just keeps adding to it."

Amelia blinked. "Is that a pony?"

Maddie laughed. "Yep. Davey's request. If Davey wants it, Ben will get it for him. I really have to watch those two."

Recognition dawned. "Oh, *this* is Davey," Amelia said, smiling at the candy-covered little boy. "I've heard a lot about you."

"Want some candy?" he asked, offering a piece of the cotton candy.

"Sure," she said, and took the small bite.

"How are the motorcycle lessons coming?" Maddie asked.

"Slowly," Amelia said.

The music stopped, and above the conversation and laughter, she heard a woman squeal, "Benny, it's been too long!"

Amelia stared after the woman as she threw herself into Ben's arms. Her stomach felt an unwelcome jolt. Dressed in leather from head to toe, the woman gave off a distinctive buzz of overt sensuality. This was *not* a good girl.

"That's Cindy. She and Ben used to be—" Maddie paused.

"Close?" Amelia mused.

"Yes," Maddie said. "Close friends."

Amelia watched the woman kiss Ben full on the

mouth and fought a wave of undiluted jealousy. Appalled at the power of her envy, she took a breath and tried to learn something from the situation. Learning had always distracted her.

She studied the woman again, her clothes, her mannerisms, her hair, her flirting manner.

"I never understood what Ben saw in her."

Amelia gave a wry laugh. "I think that's pretty easy to see. She's very sexy," she said, feeling inadequate in comparison and not liking it.

Maddie met Amelia's gaze. "She has a terrible reputation."

Amelia nodded slowly. "I wonder what she did to get it."

"You're not anything like her," Maddie assured her.

Amelia, however, didn't feel reassured. "I can see that."

"Ben would kill me for telling you this, but I'm so glad he is finally involved with someone nice," Maddie said.

"We're not really involved. He's just teaching me to ride a motorcycle."

"Uh-huh," Maddie said in disbelief and cocked her head to one side. "Can I call you for lunch sometime?"

Amelia hesitated. She wasn't at all certain of the future of her involvement with Ben. Maddie was kind, though, she reasoned. There was no reason they couldn't be friends. "Sure," she said. "That would be nice."

A few minutes later Amelia meandered closer to Ben and waved at him while he was with a customer.

He motioned for her to wait, but she smiled and said, "That's okay. I can see you're busy."

On her way home she thought about Ben. In fact, she decided she was thinking about Ben Palmer entirely too much, so she switched mental channels to the differences between good girls and bad girls. Amelia started to wonder if perhaps bad girls had more fun.

Her thoughts turned back to Ben, unsettling her further. Crazy. Ben Palmer was making her crazy. He'd become too important to her, and she needed to amend that. Drumming her fingertips on the steering wheel, she began to concoct a plan to de-crazy herself.

Six

"The best prevention for going crazy over a man is to go out with other men."

Amelia reluctantly agreed with Sherry's advice and joined "Mr. Bluechip" for a poetry reading. Although Amelia enjoyed poetry as much as the next person, two-thirds of the way through the reading her mind began to wander to images of motorcycles and minibikes and black leather.

Frowning at herself, she forced her attention away from Ben and on to the reader. They finished off the evening with coffee at a popular shop in downtown Roanoke. Amelia tried her best to make the conversation sparkle, but it was as dull as dishwater.

By the time she arrived home and fell into bed, she began to worry that Ben may have ruined her for normal men. When her heart picked up at the sound of Ben's voice-mail messages, she chided herself for her reaction and returned his calls when she was certain he wouldn't be available. Doggedly sticking to her plan, she attended a lecture with Mr. Bluechip the following night.

A philosophy professor extended an open invitation to the faculty to listen to his alternative rock band at a local club, so Amelia slipped into the back of the room and sipped a soda while she watched the mass of gyrating bodies.

"I didn't know this was your kind of music," a familiar voice said above the loud song.

Ben. Amelia's heart jumped and she nearly spilled her soda. She stole a quick glance at him, then took a careful breath. "The lead guitarist is a faculty member."

Ben frowned. "What? I didn't hear you."

Amelia raised her voice and repeated herself.

Ben nodded and leaned back against the wall. "The drummer is one of my mechanics."

Surprised, Amelia glanced at the band. "You don't say. Interesting mix."

"You've been busy this week," Ben said, his gaze on the band also.

"I try to keep busy," she said, wondering how long they would need to yell at each other to be heard above the volume of the music.

"Maddie said she talked with you."

"I met Davey. He's cute," she said, sensitive to his arm brushing hers.

"Maddie said you were around when Cindy showed up."

Amelia tensed. "Cindy, I don't believe I met her."

"She was the one who practically jumped me in front of everyone."

Amelia nodded. "Oh, yes. She was—" she searched for the right description "—eye-catching."

"She does that to everybody," Ben told her.

Amelia nodded again. Ben seemed to be waiting for her to say something more, but she could think of nothing.

"It doesn't really mean anything," he added. "We're not—"

Amelia suddenly didn't want any details. "Oh, well, that's none of my business," she said in a voice that sounded squeaky to her own ears. "I mean, you and I don't have that kind of—"

Swearing, Ben lowered his head to hers and took her arm. "Let's go outside. The music's so loud I can only hear every other word."

They stepped outside, and she drew in a quick breath of cool night air that sharpened her senses. He gently urged her against the brick outer wall of the club and put his hand beside her head, making a natural physical enclosure with his body. He was too close, and she was too aware of his strength. She was too aware of the intimacies they'd shared and the sense of unfinished business between them.

"You've been avoiding me," Ben said. "Why?"

The full force of his personality hit her head-on. Her heart hammered in her throat. Amelia swallowed a gulp. "I...uh—"

His gaze didn't waver from her face.

She bit her lip. "I thought it would be wise— It would help me keep perspective—"

He arched a dark eyebrow. "Perspective?"

"Exactly," Amelia said, knowing she'd been clear as mud.

"I think you're gonna have to clean off my windshield a little so I can understand."

Amelia would trade a month's worth of chocolate for the ability to instantly transport herself *any*where else. "Well, I started thinking about some things you've said and about the differences between bad and good. And while I'm probably not as good as you think I am, I'm also not as bad as the kind of woman to which you're accustomed. In that case, I can't really blame you for not being interested in the same way, so in order to keep my perspective, it might be best for me to—" she took a breath and finished "—keep busy."

"Are you trying to say you think you don't turn me on?"

Amelia's stomach dipped. "I suppose so," she said, then quickly went on. "It's understandable with the kind of woman you're accustomed to seeing. I'm not experienced in the same way—"

"What gave you that impression?"

Amelia's edginess turned to impatience. "I think I've expressed myself adequately. Could we talk about something else?"

"No. I want to know what made you think I don't want you."

"Because you've shown remarkable restraint," she blurted out, then crossed her arms over her chest in frustration. "I don't know why we're talking about this. You prefer a woman with a casual attitude toward intimacy and lots of experience and a strong sense of adventure and independence."

"You might have been right five years ago, but you're wrong now."

"I am not."

He looked taken aback at her flat certainty for all of a second. Then he shook his head. "You are wrong."

"I am not," she repeated, knowing their argument bore a strong resemblance to a pair of children squabbling.

His eyes narrowed in irritation. "I know what I want, Amelia. Don't push me. I wouldn't mind showing you right now."

A thrill of anticipation raced through her, and she tamped it down. "I've worked very hard to get a proper perspective on this, and I'm not going to let you confuse me again. You don't want me, and it's okay."

"Why in *hell* do you keep saying that?"

Her pride was limping. She felt vulnerable and cornered. She just prayed he couldn't see the extent of her emotions in her eyes. "Because you stopped."

Ben lifted his head and groaned as if he were in pain. "You weren't ready."

Amelia stared at him in disbelief. "I beg your pardon."

"You weren't."

Amelia reached the end of her patience. "This is ridiculous. I'm going back inside the club."

Ben blocked her. In the dim reflection of the floodlight, she thought she saw a muscle twitch in his jaw.

"Did you ever think I might have stopped because for once in my life I was trying to be something other than a selfish sonovabitch?"

"No," she said flatly, and ducked under his arm.

Ben snagged her arm as she tried to escape. "Did you ever think I might have decided I shouldn't take you just because I could?"

Amelia was afraid to even consider the possibility. She felt as if she'd been slowly building a wall, brick by brick, over the past few days. Her mortar wasn't dry and Ben could easily knock down her meager defense. She tried again to put distance between them. "No. And I don't believe in Tinker Bell, either."

Ben stared at her for a long moment, then released her arm. His nostrils flared as he inhaled quickly. "Okay."

He was going to let her go. Amelia felt both relief and crazy disappointment.

"That does it," he said, pivoting quickly, and Amelia felt the earth tilt as he tossed her over his shoulder.

Shocked speechless, she felt her stomach bounce against his hard shoulder with every step he took as she stared at his backside.

"What are you doing!" she finally managed.

"Taking you home," he told her.

"I can do that on my own. I have my own car," she said, trying to wriggle free.

"Stop squirming or you'll fall." He marched to his motorcycle.

"This is ridiculous. Insane," she continued heatedly. "You're acting like some Neanderthal caveman."

"You oughta know," Ben said with a dirty-sounding chuckle. "You've got the doctorate in history."

Amelia had never struck a person in her life, but she thought this could be a first.

Pulling her off his shoulder, he let her slide down the length of his body. His dark gaze caught hers, and despite her anger, she felt a sizzle all the way to her toes.

He reached for the helmet, and Amelia's rational brain kicked in. She turned to run.

Ben caught her and held her against the front of him. "I thought I told you the game plan," he muttered in her ear. "I'm taking you home."

"I didn't agree."

"You don't have to agree, remember? You *asked* me to kidnap you." He put the helmet on her head.

"I changed my mind," she said stiffly, feeling trapped.

Ben smiled, showing her a glimpse of his gentler side, giving her a little hope. "Tough."

Within a minute they peeled out of the parking lot. Amelia soon learned they weren't headed in the direction of her house. "I thought you said we were going home," she said loudly to him.

"We are."

He continued driving until he pulled into the driveway of a small Georgian-style house. She automatically pulled off her helmet and stared at it in confusion. "Why are we here?"

"I said we were going home," he told her, capturing her hand and tugging her toward the front door. "This is my home."

Nonplussed, she did a double take. "You're kidding."

"You were expecting a Hell's Angels hideout?"

"Not quite," she said, although that was close to the truth.

"Then what?"

She smiled sweetly. "A cave."

He shook his head and grinned. "I think I've ruined you."

"I know you have," she muttered under her breath as he led her inside to the foyer lit by a shiny brass and glass fixture. "This is beautiful," she said.

"I'll give you a tour later," he told her, putting himself against the wall, and drawing her between his legs. "We need to take care of your misunderstanding first."

Amelia's chest tightened. "It's really not—"

He put his finger over her mouth. "This time I talk and you listen."

She sighed, wondering how he made her feel like liquid fire.

"I've wanted you since the first time I saw you."

Amelia felt her heart stop.

"I take a cold shower after every time you ride with me on my bike. Do you know what it's like for me to feel your breasts against my back? Your thighs hugging mine? Your arms around my chest? And your breath on my neck?"

He slid his hands down to her bottom and gently rocked her against him, leaving her no doubt of his desire. She clung to her fading rational thoughts.

"I didn't take you the night of your husband's birthday because you weren't ready."

Amelia shook her head, but he went on.

"You weren't. You were grieving over him. I'm not a substitute," he said resolutely. "I wanted you so bad I was shaking with it. I would have taken you sitting, standing or on the floor."

He lowered his mouth to her neck and opened his lips against her skin. Amelia felt her little wall of bricks tumble. If she were the type to swear, she would do so now. Why couldn't he be less exciting to her? Less interesting? Why did her body and heart, and even her mind, respond to him so easily, when other more appropriate men left her cold? Why did she want him so much? She had thought it was because he represented everything forbidden to her, but now she was beginning to wonder.

She struggled with her confusion. "I thought I amused you."

"You do that and more," he murmured, trailing his mouth down to her chest.

"You said I was a good girl," she managed, wanting him too much.

"You are."

His voice, his words, his touch burned away her restraint. Her reserve ripped in two, her passion spilled over.

"Not that good," she said, and pulled open his shirt. His buttons bounced on the wooden floor, and Amelia sank into his chest with her hands and mouth.

Ben swore under his breath and plunged his fingers through her hair. "This is crazy," he muttered.

"Yes," she whispered, skimming her tongue over his skin. She felt his heart hammering against her cheek while her own pulse raced out of control.

"We're from different worlds," he told her.

Amelia slowly rubbed her face back and forth across his chest and followed her bold instinct. She lowered her hands to the top of his jeans.

Ben sucked in a swift breath and put his hand over hers. "Amelia," he said in a rough voice. "Be sure." He lifted her chin and gazed into her eyes. "I'm not like your husband."

At another time the sexually intent look in his gaze

would have given her pause. Instead, she felt a surge
of feminine courage. Or craziness.

"And I'm not like Cindy. I'm sure." Her eyes on
his, she lowered his zipper and took him into her
hand. "Are you?"

She stroked the full length of his hard shaft, cup-
ping and caressing him. Ben closed his eyes, and
Amelia watched in fascination as pleasure swept over
his face.

His eyes opened slightly, and he dipped his mouth
to hers, taking her with his tongue as he grew harder
and slick within her hand.

"I want to be inside you," he said against her
mouth. "Right now."

Amelia's blood pounded through all her pulse
points.

"You're wearing too many clothes," he said. In
between kisses, he removed her blouse and bra, then
slacks and panties until she stood in the foyer naked,
against him. His hardness pressed against her bare
belly like a primitive sexual promise. His chest gently
abraded the sensitive tips of her breasts as he lowered
his hand between her legs.

He found her warm and wet. Flushed, hot with
arousal, Amelia felt as if her body was screaming,
ready! She shuddered beneath his touch, her knees
dipping.

"Protection," he muttered with an oath, and lifted
his head to draw in a long breath.

Amelia shook her own head to clear it. "Protection?" she echoed.

"Right. Did you bring something?"

She blinked. It took a few seconds before she realized what he was asking. Embarrassed, she looked down. "No. I didn't think— I guess I thought you—"

He gave a rough chuckle. "I was never a Boy Scout. I don't carry it around in my back pocket."

"I haven't had a reason to carry anything in my purse."

"You do now." He slid his hand over her bare bottom and lowered his voice. "I can take care of you upstairs."

He swung her up in his arms and carried her up the steps, turning the corner into a darkened room. He flicked on a soft lamp and laid Amelia on the bed. Holding her gaze all the while, he tugged off his shirt and jacket, kicked off his shoes and ditched his jeans.

He stood before her naked, his hair mussed from her fingers and his eyes dark with passion. Everything about his body suggested power. His shoulders were broad, his abdomen hard, his thighs muscular and his sex large and swollen.

He hid nothing from her, not his body or his desire. He didn't want a quick mating under the sheets after the lights had been turned off. He would want more.

Amelia's stomach twisted in a strange mix of anticipation and apprehension. She'd had sex before. Why did she feel like this was something new? Why did she have this deep-down intuition that after tonight, she would never be the same?

He pulled a few plastic packets out of a bedside table. Before Amelia could begin to register her surroundings, he followed her down on the bed, his warm body covering hers. She touched the outline of his cobra tattoo, and fiddled with his tiny gold hoop earring.

"Are you sure you weren't a pirate in another

life?'' she whispered, disconcerted by the way her fingers trembled.

''I never thought too much about past lives,'' he said. ''I'm too busy with this one.'' His mouth explored hers again.

She felt the click of her hair clip as he released it. ''I want it loose,'' he whispered against her ear, then slid his mouth down to her breasts. He licked and sucked and nibbled at the tips of her breasts until she could barely stand the delicious tension he created.

She wiggled beneath him and moaned, squeezing his shoulders.

He slipped his hand between her thighs again and made a gruff sound of approval. ''Oh, Amelia, you're heaven and hell at the same time. I want to take you every way I can.'' He gave an unsteady laugh. ''Damn, I want to do it all at once.''

Watching her face, he eased one finger inside her. ''You're wet and tight.'' He lowered his head and dipped his tongue into her belly button while he continued to caress her.

Amelia grew more swollen and hot with each stroke.

When he lowered his head still again, she closed her eyes and felt his mouth on her intimately. He took her with his lips and tongue. His tongue was tenderly ruthless, spinning her higher and higher. Utterly consumed by him, she jerked as spasms of ecstasy shook her inside and out. She called out his name.

Ben wrapped himself around her as she continued to tremble. With his thumb, he wiped the tears from beneath her eyes. ''You okay?'' he asked.

She took a careful breath and nodded. She swallowed down the odd mix of emotion crowding her throat. "Yes."

"Good," he told her, reaching for a plastic packet. "We've just gotten started."

Seven

His words rolled through her like thunder.

She tried to catch her breath, her heart, her mind, but the way he looked at her kept her spinning.

He thrust inside her, and Amelia gave in. His invasion was physical, mental and emotional. He was large and she felt the sensation of being stretched, a momentary discomfort. Yet she wanted more.

He sucked in a sharp breath of air, his nostrils flaring. "Oh, hell, why didn't you tell me you were so tight?"

Her mouth dry from panting, she swallowed again. "I didn't know."

She experimentally undulated beneath him and watched him shudder. Growing accustomed to the sensation of him inside her, she moved again.

"If you keep moving, I'm not gonna last," he told her, taking another slow, sensual thrust inside her.

"You don't need to last," she whispered, fascinated by the intensity of his arousal. She moved her hips in rhythmic counterpoint to his, some instinct driving her to send him over the top. She didn't want him holding back.

He thrust deeper, his body straining. "I want it to last," he said in a rough voice, his eyes black with need.

"You don't need to last," she whispered again, her own body beginning to spiral upward. "This isn't the last time."

Her words seemed to blast through his control, and he plunged inside her in earnest. He felt like lightning, thunder and rain, and everything alive and powerful. Pumping inside her, he took her, pushing her over the edge just before he shuddered with his own long, hot release.

They didn't say anything for several moments. Ben was relieved because he had no clue what to say. She tucked her head beneath his chin, and within moments, her breath whispered in a sweet, easy rhythm against his throat.

He felt a strange tightening in the region of his heart that spread to his chest and then the rest of his body. Carefully disentangling himself, he got out of bed and walked to the window.

Raking his hand through his hair, he took a deep breath and began to pace. He abruptly stopped when he remembered he didn't pace. He was *not* a pacer.

It was just sex, he told himself. Great sex. But just sex. So why had it felt different?

He rubbed his face. It hadn't been different. It had

just seemed different because Amelia was so different.

He swore under his breath in disgust. He had the brains of a chicken right now, and his thoughts could have fertilized an entire farm. He struggled with the opposing urges to protect Amelia and run like hell.

Sucking in another deep breath, he rolled his shoulders. They hadn't made any promises, he reminded himself. Amelia understood he wasn't the forever type, and he understood he'd never fit into her world.

The truth calmed him. He brushed off an odd niggling of dissatisfaction with his thoughts. Glancing back at Amelia as she lay curled in his bed, he felt the familiar urgency she'd fired in him since the first time he'd seen her.

He returned to bed and pulled her into his arms. This wouldn't last forever. They wouldn't want each other with the same kind of fever. That was okay, he thought. Until the fever cooled, he would take his fill, and he suspected she would, too.

When Amelia awakened, she stared straight into a muscular male chest. She blinked, quickly realizing she was naked. Disoriented, she blinked again, and her body reminded her that she had made love with Ben and she was in his bed.

Stiffly flipping over on her back, she looked at the ceiling. Uncertainty swelled within her. She felt confused and self-conscious. She knew she'd been incredibly brazen with Ben. Given the same situation, she'd probably behave the same way again. She couldn't recall how many times they'd made love. The night had become a passionate blur of giving and taking, as if they couldn't get enough of each other.

Her breasts were tender beneath the crisp cotton sheets, her skin sensitive to the very air in the room. She had never been so thoroughly taken. She didn't feel used, but she did feel incredibly vulnerable.

Heat suffused her skin from head to toe. She wanted to cover herself, get dressed and run away. She wanted to roll over and make love to Ben again.

Amelia glanced at the alarm clock and remembered she was in the middle of a workweek. Opting for clothes, she carefully scooted out of bed and searched for her underwear. Her brain moving at the speed of a snail, she finally remembered her clothes were downstairs in the foyer.

Stealing down the steps, she located her panties. It took her three tries to pull them on without falling down. With trembling hands, she quickly gathered her other clothes together.

"Going somewhere?"

Amelia's heart shot into her throat at the sound of Ben's voice. She jerked her head toward him. With his arms crossed over his bare chest, he leaned against the banister dressed in nothing but denim and an intent gaze.

She scooped up her clothes and tried to make her brain work. "I remembered tomorrow—" she glanced at his grandfather clock, noting the predawn time "—today," she corrected, "is a workday and I'll need my car."

He pushed away from the banister and came down the rest of the steps. His dark hair was mussed, his eyes heavy-lidded from lovemaking and sleep. Killer sexy. "How were you planning to get your car?"

Amelia hugged her blouse against her chest. "I hadn't gotten that far." Why did she feel so nervous, she wondered. She managed a laugh and shook her head. "I thought I did well to find my clothes."

He reached out a hand to touch her hair. "Regrets?"

Amelia took a breath and answered honestly. "No. Nerves."

"Are you sore?"

"No," she quickly said, denying the tiny ache between her legs. "A little," she conceded at his skeptical expression.

Tugging gently on her hair, he urged her toward him. "Come here."

Amelia dropped her clothes and walked into his arms. Her bare breasts meshed with his chest while he held her close. His embrace melted her. She could stay here forever. She could almost believe he wanted her to stay. Dangerous notions, she thought, and made herself gather her wits.

"Would you give me a raincheck on the house tour?" she asked.

He nuzzled her hair and slid his hands down to cup her bottom. "You sure I can't talk you into coming back to bed with me?"

Amelia sighed and felt her heart turn over. "I'm sure you can," she said. "But I think I should go." She hoped he wouldn't make her explain further. It was going to take some time for her to pull herself together enough to present her morning lecture.

"Okay," he said, slowly releasing her. "Give me a minute to get dressed."

Her heart tripping double time, Amelia used that moment to struggle into her own clothes. When he helped her onto his motorcycle and drove away from his house, the cold air should have helped clear her mind, but it didn't. She decided Ben had made love to her until her brains took a hike. She just hoped her condition wasn't permanent.

He pulled into the deserted parking lot next to her car, and Amelia pulled off her helmet.

"You're quiet," he said, walking with her to her car.

She shrugged. "I'm not sure what to say. I've never really done this—" Her cheeks heated at his doubtful expression. "Well, I haven't ever done it this way."

His lips quirked into a half grin. "'This way.' Does that mean you haven't been on top? Or you stopped after three times instead of five? Or—"

Groaning, she shook her head and held up her hand for him to stop. "You're not helping! The etiquette for this situation completely escapes me."

"Etiquette?" he echoed. His grin faded. "Forget Emily Post. What's on your mind, Miss Amelia?"

She dipped her head. "My mind feels empty and full at the same time. I feel like I still want to be close to you," she said, stealing a glance at him. "I—" She saw his jaw tighten and took a deep breath. "I think I'd better stop while I'm ahead." She bit her lip. "Thank you for, uh, a mind-blowing night."

She focused on unlocking her car door. He covered her unsteady hand with his, so solid and strong. "I'll call you," he said in a low voice next to her ear.

"Sure," she said, but couldn't quite keep the disbelief from her voice. Before she could blink, he whirled her around.

"I want you again," he told her, his gaze intent.

Her chest tightened. "You're not helping unmuddle my mind."

"I like you muddled," he said, then muddled her mind further by kissing her.

"What's that you're whistling, Mr. Palmer?" Greg Wade, his newest salesman asked, poking his head through the door.

Ben abruptly stopped perusing sales figures for the month and shook his head at himself. He hadn't realized he'd been whistling until Greg pointed it out.

"It sounded kinda like Hootie and the Blowfish," Greg said. "The sales reports must look pretty good if you're whistling."

"They're good," Ben said, but he suspected the reason he was whistling had more to do with a certain history professor, whose mind he enjoyed muddling.

"So, you're in a good mood?" Greg continued.

Leaning back in his chair, Ben swallowed a chuckle. He knew where this was heading. Three other employees had visited him this afternoon. "Yeah. I'm not eating glass today."

Greg squared his shoulders. "Well, I was wondering if I could have a raise. I met my quota every week except—"

Ben smiled and shook his head. "No."

Greg's face fell. "No?"

"No, but after you beat your quota for the next four weeks, ask me again."

Greg scratched his chin for a moment, then nodded. "Okay. I'll be back in four weeks."

Ben watched the salesman stride out of his office with a renewed kick of purpose. Ben had always known he didn't have a sales personality. He was too damn blunt. Consequently he surrounded himself with terrific sales performers. In the past couple of years, he'd figured out what made these guys tick. They needed someone to raise the bar, then provide the reward. It was the same way he'd once felt about stunt driving. He'd always wanted to try a more difficult stunt. The reward had been the thrill of succeeding. His problem, however, had been the diminishing thrill.

If someone had tried to tell him ten years ago that stunt driving would get old, he would have said they were crazy. Within the past few years, however, breaking a few bones and nearly breaking his neck just to pop a wheelie a few inches higher didn't give him the same kick. His sister, Maddie, said his waning obsession with risk was a sign of maturity. Ben had snorted at her theory, just as he continued to snort at her suggestion that he change the make and model of the women he dated.

He would rather drink oil than admit it, but maybe Maddie had more on the ball than he'd thought. Glancing at his phone, he remembered making love to Amelia last night. All day, the sweet, sensual picture of her hadn't been far from his mind. The sounds of her sighs and moans played over his nerve endings. The one-second image of the expression on her face when he'd plunged inside her had the power to make him hard.

A twinge of unease prickled under his skin.

It wasn't permanent, he reminded himself. Maddie might be right about a few things, but she was totally wrong about him and marriage.

Plus, there was the matter of the recent offer he'd received for the dealership. Selling the business would give him the opportunity to regain some of his freedom. He would finally be able to hit the road for that cross-country trip he'd always wanted to take.

His mind slipped back to Amelia. Their relationship wasn't permanent, but it was the best damn temporary thing that had happened to him in a long time. He eyed the phone again and picked it up to call her.

Three hours later, Ben turned onto Amelia's street with a vaguely unsettled feeling. He'd called Amelia several times and only connected with her answering machine. As he drove closer to her house, his vaguely unsettled feeling kicked into fourth gear at the sight of a BMW in her driveway.

A man dressed in preppy clothes bearing flowers stood on her doorstep. Ben thought about the little surprise he'd bought her and scowled. He'd been convinced she was vulnerable and inexperienced. That little witch, he thought, remembering the guileless innocence on her face. He wondered how many men she was playing the same way.

Hot anger burned like a coal in his gut. He was tempted to leave her in the dust, but her deceit rankled him enough that he wanted to make her sweat. Pulling to a stop in front of her house, he dismounted from the bike and walked to the front porch where Mr. BMW continued to stand.

"Ben Palmer," he said, extending his hand.

As the man gave him a careful once-over, Ben realized why the guy was still on the porch. Amelia's CD player was blasting out Sheryl Crow. Ben leaned on the doorbell.

"I've been ringing the doorbell once every two minutes. I'm Edwin Carter. Amelia and I attended a poetry reading."

"Is that so?" Ben grinned, feeling the devil rise within him. "I'm teaching her to ride a motorcycle."

The man's eyes widened in surprise. "A motorcycle," he repeated.

"Yep. She's a tiger, isn't she?" He banged on the door and began to yell. "Amelia! Answer the door!"

After repeated banging, the volume of the CD decreased and Amelia swung open the door. Her hair was tied in a high ponytail, and she wore a white shirt splattered with paint. She blinked at the sight of the two men on her front porch. She looked so stunned he *almost* felt sorry for her. Almost.

"I tried ringing the doorbell," Edwin said apologetically.

"Edwin, Ben," she said in a weak voice and stood aside. "Come in."

Ben grinned. "You sound surprised, darlin'."

Her cheeks bloomed with color. "I've been painting my bedroom. I must have lost track of the time."

"I brought you roses," Edwin said.

Amelia gave a smile that looked more like a cringe. "They're lovely," she said as she accepted the flowers. "Um, can I speak with you on the porch for a moment? Excuse me, Ben," she said, then hurried out front with Edwin.

Cooling his heels for a moment, Ben reconsidered the conclusions he'd drawn about Amelia. She had appeared genuinely surprised. Still, a guy didn't show up with roses without some encouragement.

Amelia reappeared with the flowers, but without Edwin.

The look of dismay on her face took some of the sting out of his irritation. Until he looked at those damn roses again. "Roses," Ben said. "You must have cranked his engine."

"I can't imagine how," she said, walking to the kitchen and pulling a vase from the cabinet beneath the sink. "I only went out with him twice."

Ben followed her. "You don't give yourself enough credit, Amelia. How many men can you play at one time?"

She slowly turned around. "'Play at one time,'" she echoed. "That sounds insulting."

He shrugged. "Hey, you got two of us to your front door at the same time tonight."

Her eyes narrowed. "Because neither of you called first."

"I called and got your answering machine. Maybe Mr. BMW did too."

Realization crossed her face. "It must have been the music. I turned my CD player up when I stirred the paint."

"Uh-huh," Ben said without a drop of sympathy or understanding. "You didn't answer my question about how many you're playing."

A tinge of anger flashed in her eyes and she walked around him. "I'm looking for your club."

"My what?"

"Your club. You're doing your caveman routine again. I'm not *playing* with anyone," she told him, her Southern drawl sharpening with precision. "You've made it perfectly clear that you don't intend anything permanent with me and that I shouldn't count on you, so I wouldn't think you'd give a Harley-Davidson damn who I see."

"Well, that's where you're wrong, Miss Amelia,"

he said moving closer to her. "I want exclusive rights."

Amelia was so upset she wanted to crack the crystal vase over his thick head. Strangely enough, at the same time, his possessiveness excited her. She understood the primal feeling, because she felt the same way about him. "The only way you get exclusive rights is by mutual agreement," she said, unable to keep her volume down.

"Okay," he growled, putting his hands on either side of the counter behind her. His eyes were dark and serious. "Consider it a done deal."

Amelia blinked in surprise. "Pardon?"

A muscle in his jaw twitched, revealing his frustration. "Consider it done. How long are you gonna leave Edwin out there on the front porch? Don't you need to tell him to go home?"

Nonplussed, Amelia took a quick breath and inhaled his scent, which only served to muddle her mind again. "I already did. I told him I'd made a previous date with you." She frowned and shook her head. "If I were a different woman, I could see other men and you the same time. And that would probably be the smartest way to keep my sanity, but I just can't be your lover and—"

"Amelia, what in hell are you talking about?"

"I'm trying to prevent going crazy over you!" she yelled.

Ben's lips lifted in a ghost of a grin and he lowered his head. "What if I want you crazy for me?"

Her heart hammered against her rib cage. "No, you said—"

His mouth took hers and stole her protest. His

closeness reminded her that she'd missed him all day long. Amelia sank against him, kissing him back.

He drew slightly away and murmured against her lips, ''What if I'm a little crazy for you?''

Eight

Within an hour, Ben helped Amelia finish painting, and they sat on the sofa polishing off a snack of sandwiches and soda.

"What made you choose red paint?" he asked, wondering how she managed to look elegant wearing an oversize, paint-stained shirt, a ponytail that was falling and a smudge of mustard on the side of her mouth.

"It isn't really red," Amelia told him, making the mustard disappear with a delicate swipe from her napkin. "It's cranberry."

"Okay," he said, swallowing a comment about how women can take a perfectly respectable color like red and rename it something prissy like cranberry. "What made you choose 'cranberry'?"

"Well, it was either that or dye my hair or trade in my car or buy all new clothes."

Horrified, he nearly choked on his soda. "Dye your hair?"

She nodded. "Yes, but I couldn't decide if I should cut it, too. I remembered—"

"Wait a minute. Cut it, too?"

She nodded.

"Don't do that."

She tilted her head and looked at him. "You're not one of those men who tries to tell women what to wear and how to fix their hair, are you?"

"I don't try," he said, unable to resist goading her.

Her eyes widened. "Oh, so you just give a royal decree and it's followed without question?"

He tugged her resisting body onto his lap. "Royal decrees are more up your alley. I just state my preferences and—"

Amelia groaned and shook her head.

"And pull out my club," he said and chuckled. "So don't cut your hair." He pulled her hair loose from the falling ponytail. "It's pretty, sexy," he said. "I like it. I like seeing you wearing nothing but your hair."

Her expression softened. "Maybe you don't need a club after all."

The sensual light in her eyes shimmied through his nerve endings. "Speaking of wearing nothing but your hair," he began.

"I didn't finish telling you why I chose cranberry paint instead of cutting my hair," she said.

Distracted by his growing arousal, but curious, he sighed. "Okay. Why?"

"I remembered reading an article in the paper that suggested if you're going to make a trendy paint change, to just paint one wall. I wanted to do something wild and impetuous.''

He swallowed a chuckle. "So you painted one wall of your bedroom red.''

"Cranberry.''

He raised an eyebrow.

She lifted her chin. "Okay. Go ahead and laugh, but it's your fault.''

Ben rolled his eyes. "I can't wait to hear the logic behind this.''

She gently pointed at his chest with her forefinger. "If you hadn't made love to me last night, then I wouldn't feel this way.''

"And what way is that?''

"Like a bottle of champagne that's been shaken up,'' she said, her expression growing serious. She glanced away as if she felt self-conscious. "Like someone replaced the old, scratched lens on my camera with a crystal-clear new one.''

The combination of her vulnerability and honesty squeezed his heart like a vise. He'd never known a woman could possess both. He'd never known how seductive the combination could be. She put into words how she felt about him, but Ben couldn't begin to do the same with his feelings for her.

"Are you trying to muddle my mind?'' he asked, nudging her head upward so he could see her eyes.

"Fat chance,'' she said with an unsteady smile.

"I didn't bring you roses,'' he told her.

"Oh, that's okay. I really don't expect—''

"I brought you something else.''

She lifted her eyebrows. "Oh, really. What?''

He grabbed his jacket from the back of the sofa

and pulled the paper sack from the pocket. "Oranges. You said you like oranges."

Her eyes grew shiny, and she swallowed. "That was thoughtful. Very thoughtful. How can I thank you?"

"Share one with me," he said.

"Yes," she agreed, and kissed him full on the mouth. It was a sweet, yet seductive caress that made him want her again. Drawing back, she began to unbutton his shirt. "Can you stay awhile?"

He could stay through the next millennium if she kept looking at him that way. "Yeah, and I came prepared this time, Amelia."

She lowered her mouth to his chest and kissed him. "Good."

Ben was amazed at how quickly his arousal went from idle to superspeed. He pulled off her clothes, and she helped him out of the rest of his, and soon her hands were sliding over his shoulders and her soft, slim legs were rubbing against his.

It would have been easy just to slide inside her wetness, to fill her up and let her milk him into ecstasy. It would have taken mere moments. The pleasure would be intense, but he sensed the satisfaction would be fleeting.

If Ben wanted satisfaction, then he would need to savor Amelia. Reining in his urgent need to be inside her, he took a deep breath and smelled the citrusy scent of the oranges.

He grinned and snagged a piece of the fruit headed for the folds of the sofa. "We forgot the orange."

Her eyes heavy-lidded and smoky with desire, she lifted her gaze to his in confusion. "Huh?"

She looked so sexy he felt like beating his chest

and letting out a primal yell. Instead, he backed
slightly away and peeled the orange.

She pushed her hair from her face. "What are you
doing?"

"Feeding you an orange," he told her, pulling off
a section and gently pushing it past her stunned lips.

Her eyes widened and she automatically bit down
on the fruit. A drop of juice slid down her chin. She
quickly reached for it, but Ben stopped her.

"Nuh-uh," he said. "I'll get it." He leaned down
and skimmed his tongue over her chin.

Holding her gaze, he took a bite of another section,
and the juice dripped to her chest.

She gave a little jerk at the sensation. "Are you
really going to—"

Answering her unfinished question, Ben lowered
his mouth to her breasts, sipping at the combined fla-
vors of orange and Amelia. He worried her nipple
with his tongue and teeth until it was a tight bead and
she was arching against his lips. She was hot, and the
scent and taste of her went to his head like a straight
shot of whiskey.

"This isn't fair," she managed around a gasp.
"You're having all the fun."

He turned his attention to her other nipple and
chuckled despite the undiluted arousal rushing
through him. "I am?"

"Yes-s-s," she hissed and pushed him away. "You
said we were going to share." Her shyness burned to
cinders, she took the orange from his hand and lifted
sections to his mouth and hers. Her hair skimming
over him with a seductive caress, she deliberately
sank lower on his torso, dripping tiny droplets on his

abdomen. Slowly, she dipped her tongue into his belly button. "My turn."

Three of the grown-up members of the Bad Boys Club popped the tops on their beers in near unison as they slouched on the comfortable furniture in Ben's den. The oak sofa table was covered with plates full of club sandwiches, nachos and cookies. The wide-screen TV displayed the ongoing rivalry between the Dallas Cowboys and the Washington Redskins.

"I've missed this," Nick Nolan, an attorney from Richmond said. "I'm usually so busy on a case I forget how great it is to have some beers and watch a football game with the guys."

"Well, you're definitely in no-woman's-land at Ben's house," Stan said. "I think the only female he lets through his hallowed door is his sister, Maddie."

An instant visual of Amelia wrapped around him in his foyer and then in his bed hit him. Ben nursed his beer and propped his feet on an ottoman. "That's a slight exaggeration."

"Oh, so you've brought 'the Biter' home with you?" Stan razzed him with a wicked grin.

"The Biter?" Nick echoed, tearing his attention from the TV.

"My lips are sealed," Ben said, thinking Amelia would be completely mortified to know she'd been referred to as the Biter.

"Aw, come on," Stan said. "Maddie says she's different from your usual type. She bites men instead of beer-bottle caps."

"Bites men?" Nick asked.

"How would you like some goat cheese on the transmission of your new car?" Ben asked.

Stan made a face. "Ooh. I hit a sore spot, and I was sure you were invulnerable to women. You and Nick were gonna be bachelors forever."

"I am," Nick said with complete confidence.

"I am," Ben agreed. His fate was sealed. He'd always known he was a nonconformist, and nonconformists didn't make great marriage partners. Especially to a history professor that had L-A-D-Y written on her from head to toe.

"I don't know, Ben," Nick said as he grabbed a cookie from the plate. "Your chocolate chip cookies are terrific. You'd make a terrific wife if you didn't have a snake tattoo."

Ben snatched the cookie from Nick's hand just as the lawyer opened his mouth. *"Wife?"*

"Uh-oh, you've lost your sense of humor." Nick narrowed his eyes. "This lady must be under your skin. Careful, Ben. Women are like ticks. Once they get their bloodsucking tentacles in your skin, it takes surgery or fire to get them out."

"If it's the right woman, you don't mind," Stan said. "You might even like it."

Groaning in unison, Nick and Ben threw nachos at Stan.

Stan crunched one of the chips and wagged his finger at them. "Say what you want, you poor saps. But I go to bed every night with a beautiful intelligent woman who makes the sun rise every morning for me. It makes all the difference in the world knowing she'll stick with me no matter what."

Nick gave a loud snort, then jumped to his feet. "Interception Redskins!"

"What?" Stan jerked his head toward the screen.

Ben caught the instant replay. His brain, however,

was stuck on Stan's words. For a moment he imagined what it might be like if Amelia were a permanent part of his life—to take her to bed and wake up beside her every morning.

Why would he want a woman cluttering his life? He was happy alone.

The accessibility held some appeal. He could inhale her scent and touch her soft skin anytime. He could make her blush or make her laugh anytime. He could goad her into a fun and crazy battle-of-the-sexes skirmish anytime. He could just *look* at her anytime.

Ben frowned at his wayward thoughts. Who was he kidding? Having a woman under his feet all the time would make him so itchy he'd want to crawl out of his own skin. It would only take a little while before she drove him nuts and he frustrated the hell out of her.

Nope, he told himself. Reality bites, but he was not wired for domestic bliss. It was best for everyone to accept that as an indisputable fact.

Amelia knocked on Ben's front door, then nervously lifted her hand to smooth her just-cut hair. Although she'd reconsidered doing the deed several times, years of fighting with her hair had made her go under the scissors. She also hadn't liked the insidious thought that Ben might not be as attracted to her if she cut it. If Ben didn't like her as she was, or as she was becoming, then she would simply have to take that chance.

He opened the door and opened his mouth, but for several seconds no sound came out.

He finally clamped his mouth shut and nodded. "You cut your hair."

"Yes," she said, lifting her chin.

"You disobedient wench," he told her. "It looks great."

Amelia felt a ridiculous surge of happiness. She beamed and stood on tiptoe to kiss him. "Thanks, Conan."

He slid his arm around her and deepened the kiss until her head began to spin.

"Uncle Ben, can I have another cookie?" a child's voice called from inside the house.

Ben pulled back with a reluctant expression on his face. "That'll have to hold me for a while. Davey's here. Joshua talked Maddie into a one-night getaway before a horse show tomorrow," he said, then yelled, "No more cookies, Davey. We gotta eat dinner first."

"Oh, what a nice surprise," Amelia said, walking through the doorway. "I get *two* men for the evening. Hi, Davey."

Ben watched Davey flash a beginner's lady-killer grin. "Hi 'melia. Ben says you're a babe."

Amelia tossed an amused glance over her shoulder. "Oh, really?"

Ben scowled. "He wasn't supposed to repeat that."

"Will Maddie kill you for teaching him about babes?"

"She'll try," Ben said. "Let me get the chicken off the grill."

"Grill? In November?"

Ben thumped his chest. "Us savage types like fire any time of the year." He turned to Davey. "Right, bud?"

"*Right!*" Davey yelled.

Ben served the chicken at the pine table in his kitchen. Although Amelia was dressed casually in slacks and a soft sweater and ate the messy barbecued chicken with her fingers, she still looked elegant. While she and Davey charmed each other, he watched her and tried to figure out how she managed it. Pretty without much paint. Quietly captivating.

She was the kind of woman who didn't overpower at first glance, he mused. But the more he looked, the more he had a tough time looking away. There was something about the engaging expression on her face when she was listening that drew him, like a light in the darkness, to her. She would deny that she was a flirt, but the way she laughed and shyly dropped her gaze grabbed his gut every time. The kick of sexy defiance combined with all that Southern femininity brought out a primitive need inside him to claim her. He wondered if she would be appalled. Dangerous thoughts, he thought uneasily.

"I'm cold," Davey said with a little shiver. He leaned against Amelia, and she gently rubbed his forehead.

"Here," she said, wrapping her arm around him. Then she frowned. "Maybe a blanket on the sofa would help."

Davey nodded, then looked at Ben. "Can I have another cookie now?"

Ben chuckled. "Yeah. You ready for the video?"

Davey nodded again and headed for the couch in the den.

"We were going to watch the big-wheel truck races," Ben told Amelia, "but in deference to you, we're watching a Disney flick."

Amelia's lips twitched. "I'm touched that you would deprive yourself of such a consciousness-expanding experience as a big-wheel truck race just for me."

Ben shook his head. "You know, your mouth has changed a lot since we first met."

She stood and leaned closer to him. "Your fault," she whispered.

Ben felt his temperature rise. "How's that?"

"You kissed it," she said, moving still closer, then teasing him by backing away.

Ben snagged her wrist and pulled her back against him, quickly taking her mouth. She felt warm and right in his arms. "Are you deliberately trying to tease the hell out of me because Davey's here and I can't do anything about it at the moment?"

Her eyes widened. "Me? A tease?"

"Yes, you," he muttered. "You better stop, or there'll be hell to pay when I get you alone."

She arched an eyebrow. "Stop what?"

Ben thought about that for a minute, then gave a wry chuckle. "Breathing," he said. "Take a seat in the den. I'll be in there in a minute."

"Let me help with the dishes."

"Nah, you'll just start breathing again and distract me."

She shook her head, still smiling. "Conan does the dishes. Should I take a picture for posterity?"

He snapped the dish towel in the air like a whip. "I have many talents."

Her eyes deepened with sensual knowledge. "I know," she said softly, and sashayed into the den.

Ben watched after her for a long moment, then snapped the dish towel again to wake himself up. He sure as hell wasn't going to stand there gawking after Amelia. Shaking his head at himself, he attacked the dishes. It only took a few minutes to load the dishwasher and right the kitchen.

By the time he poked his head around the corner to the den, however, Amelia was sitting on the couch with Davey curled up in her lap. She alternated between glancing at the Disney flick and gazing down at Davey as she stroked his forehead.

Leaning against the wall, he watched her. She looked natural with a child on her lap, as if she were born to nurture, as if her instinct to love were ingrained.

His mind traveled a step further and he saw Amelia, her eyes smiling with joy, full and heavy with child. His child. His heart swelled at the onslaught of emotions that hammered him. She would be so excited. He would be overprotective. It would be an adventure, and they would share every moment of it.

"Ben? Something wrong?" Amelia asked, breaking into his thoughts.

It took him a moment to move from his hazy visual to reality. When he realized he'd been thinking of Amelia as the mother of his child, his gut twisted into a triple knot. He bit back an oath. A *father!* He had never wanted to be a *father*. He had, in fact, always been damn careful never to become a *father*.

Amelia continued to look at him with a gentle, concerned expression on her face.

Ben gazed at her in suspicion. This classy, genteel woman was making him think crazy thoughts.

She must be a witch.

Nine

"**W**hen is my next motorcycle driving lesson?"
Amelia asked Ben the following weekend.

Sprawled beside her in his big bed, naked, with his
eyes closed, he reminded her of a panther at rest. He
opened his eyes slightly. "Soon," he said, and closed
his eyes.

She propped her head on her elbow and skimmed
her fingertips over his chest. "*Soon* is vague."

Sighing, he took her hand and lifted it to his lips.
"You've spent the past twelve hours wearing me out
and you want to know when your next lesson is," he
grumbled.

"Yep," she said cheerfully. "How can I prove to
you that I'm not a sissy if I don't learn to ride your
big, black bike?"

He opened his eyes and arched his eyebrows.
"Ride my big, black bike?" He chuckled low and

dirty. "There are many ways I could interpret that, but something you need to remember is that you won't be driving *my* bike. I'll start you out on a dirt bike—"

"Why?"

"In a field," he continued.

"Why?"

"So when you fall over, you won't hurt yourself too much."

"Oh," Amelia said, disliking the image of herself buried beneath a motorcycle. "My balance has improved since I was a child, so I shouldn't fa—"

"Trust me," he told her. "Everyone falls."

Amelia thought about that for a moment.

Ben slid his hands over her torso, distracting her. "Second thoughts?" he asked in a mild tone. "Sissy," he added, then began to tickle her.

Annoyed, Amelia laughed despite herself. "Stop! You're terrible!" she said, shrieking when he continued to tickle. "Mean! You're cruel and horrid and—"

His mouth landed firmly on hers, cutting off her insults. He eased one hand upward to cup her breast and toy with her nipple. Her bones went soft from his touch, but Amelia was determined to give him a piece of her mind. His caveman practice of kissing her so she would bend to his will was ridiculous. Her head began to spin. She was going to fix him good when he stopped. She would—

The phone rang, and he pulled back.

Both of them stared at each other, breathing hard through three rings.

"You're a jerk," she finally managed without nearly as much heat as she'd intended. "Are you going to get that?"

He finally picked up the phone. "Yes," he said into the receiver. After a moment he smiled. "Ah, hello, Jenna Jean."

A woman, she realized, and felt an ugly twist in her stomach. Suddenly, acutely aware of the fact that she was naked in Ben's bed while he was talking to another woman, Amelia decided this was a good time to get dressed. She turned to get out of bed, but was stopped by Ben's hand around her wrist.

She glanced at him and watched him shake his head at her. She shook her head in disagreement and attempted to pry his fingers loose.

"Sounds good, Jenna. I'll see if I can make it and get back to you."

He was making a date? Amelia buried a fingernail in his hand and scooted closer to the edge of the bed.

"Ouch!" Ben glared at Amelia and reached for her ankle. "Uh, no, Jenna. It was just my cat. I need to get her declawed," he said meaningfully.

"You want me to bring my new what?" he asked, his voice rising a half octave. He swore. "She wouldn't be interested in meeting a bunch of weirdos like you."

Amelia paused in her struggle to escape. The conversation had taken an interesting turn.

"No, dammit. I am not afraid she'll learn the truth about me from you."

He gave a fierce frown. "Yeah, well, my cookies are better than yours, anyway. You tell your sorry husband to watch out for the big cheese."

Then he hung up the phone and glowered at Amelia.

"Jenna Jean?" she prompted.

"Jenna Jean Anderson Michaels. I've known her

since I was a kid. She's married to one of my *former* good friends, Stan Michaels. They just invited us to dinner," he said with a scowl.

Confused, Amelia studied him. "You said something about her cookies. Is she a bad cook?"

Ben snorted and tossed aside the covers, rising from the bed. "Bad cook? An overachiever like Jenna? She's a good cook, but she hates it that my cookies *are* better than hers."

Amelia sat up and pulled the sheet up with her. "So you've eaten dinner with them before?"

"Of course," he said as he paced the length of the bedroom.

"Then why don't you want us to eat dinner with them?"

"They want to meet you," he said. "They want to inspect you and drill you and poke at you. They want to see if you're real."

Still confused, Amelia shrugged. "If they're your friends, I'm sure they wouldn't be unkind to me."

"No, they wouldn't be unkind," he conceded. He shook his head, looking distracted. "I just don't want to bring them into this."

Her stomach tightened at his evasive tone. Amelia was quiet for a moment. She knew she wasn't the kind of woman he regularly dated. An uneasy feeling of not measuring up nudged through her. "Are you concerned I would embarrass you?"

Ben jerked his head away from the window to look at her. "Hell, no."

She adjusted the sheet over her again. "Then why don't you want me to meet your friends? There must be something—"

"No—" He crossed the room in seconds and rejoined her on the bed. "It's nothing like that. I don't want them horning in with a lot of nosy questions."

"Like what?"

He covered her fidgeting hands with his and sighed. "Relationship questions. Questions about the future." He tugged her into his arms and gave a wry grin. "I'm a selfish sonovabitch. I don't want to share you. I want you for me and me for you," he said, kissing her. "And I don't want anyone else's opinion."

Amelia wrapped her arms around him and felt her heart contract painfully. She heard his unspoken thoughts and feelings. *We're not right for each other. I don't know how long this will last.*

Fighting the confusing sting of tears on the inside of her eyelids, she tried to concentrate on here and now. Here and now, Ben held her as if he wanted her more than anything, as if he would never let go. But Amelia was too much of a realist to believe that "here and now" would last forever.

The weekend before Thanksgiving, Ben picked up Amelia for a charity motorcycle run for the homeless. She felt his once-over through the three layers of clothes she wore.

"Miss Amelia, you *almost* look like a motorcycle mama," he teased. "Look at you. Black jeans and black suede boots." He slid his finger just under the neckline of her sweater. "If you weren't wearing a pink cashmere sweater and a rose-colored quilted jacket—"

"I'd freeze."

"No black leather jacket yet?"

She looked at him sideways. "Evel Knievel was getting his cleaned, so I couldn't borrow his."

Ben chuckled and pulled her against him. "When I first met you, you were a sweet and gentle-spoken woman. I've ruined your mouth."

"Think so?" She brushed her lips over his, feeling bold and natural at the same time. "I don't mind what you've done to my mouth. I don't mind what you've done to me," she said, watching him watch her, his undiluted attention capturing hers.

Yet. An unsettling thought of what he could do to her and her heart made her draw back. "I raised some money for the charity run," she said. When she'd asked, Ben had explained to her that the charity run requested one fee for the drivers and an additional fee for passengers.

He looked surprised. "I told you that you didn't have to do that. I had your fee covered at the dealership."

"I like to hold up my end," she said, lifting her chin slightly.

He nodded thoughtfully, almost admiringly. "I bet you always have," he said, then caught her hand. "Let's get moving."

The motorcyclists met in the Market Square in downtown Roanoke, and Amelia couldn't help thinking the large group reminded her of a Hell's Angels convention. It was a wonderful paradox that all these people were here for the sake of charity. Several participants wore armbands that said Hogs for the Homeless, which Ben translated for her as Harley Riders for the Homeless.

After a few speeches from the mayor and event organizers, the riders revved up and began the run. Since they would be riding for a while, Ben had installed minimicrophones so they could talk. Just before she wrapped her arms around him, Amelia had glanced in dismay at the number of eateries listed on the program where they were scheduled to stop.

"Are we supposed to eat at all these restaurants?"

Ben chuckled. "No. We'll stop at all of them, but the idea is that we create such a spectacle that other people will come out and look at us. While they're gawking, they buy food and some of the proceeds will go to the cause. Nice trick, huh?"

"Yes, it is. I see a lot of the participants waving at you. How many of these runs have you done?"

He shrugged. "I dunno. A dozen or so. It's easy. It's for a good cause. No big deal."

She smiled, pressing her face into his shoulder. "Better watch out, or everyone will learn your secret."

"What's that?"

"Underneath that leather jacket beats the heart of a responsible, hardworking, generous citizen."

"They'll never believe you," he told her. "And that's fine with me."

After a few stops Amelia grew quiet and closed her eyes.

"No sleeping allowed," Ben said.

She smiled and shook her head. "How did you know? Do you have eyes in the back of your head?"

"Your body relaxed," he told her, then added wryly, "I'm very aware of your body. Start singing."

Amelia blinked. "Pardon?"

"I said sing."

At a loss, she stared at the back of his neck. "Why?"

"Because I am the master of this bike. I rule."

She laughed. "Try again, Conan."

"Because it will keep you awake," he said. "And I want to hear you sing to me."

Her heart tightened and Amelia had the unsettling sense that she would do just about anything for Ben. Not wise, she thought, for a temporary man. "What if I have a terrible singing voice?"

"You don't," he said. "In your photo album, there were a bunch of pictures of you in group chorus pictures."

Amelia cringed. "That was a long time ago."

"Just like riding a bike. You never forget."

A sinking sensation inside her told her he wasn't going to let up. "Okay, hop in anytime," she said, and belted out "Row, Row, Row Your Boat."

Ben grumbled, but joined in for a few rounds. Amelia exhausted her repertoire of rounds, then, giving in to an attack of silliness, she made him Name That Tune while she mimicked Prince's "Kiss."

"When did a nice girl like you learn to sing such a wicked song?"

"I sneaked off and listened to his cassettes on my Walkman when I was a teenager. My mother thought I was listening to opera for music appreciation class. For a while it was one of my secret fantasies to be one of those bad-girl dancers in his music videos."

"I'm shocked," Ben said, through a chuckle. "What would your mother say?"

"She would faint," Amelia told him, amused by the thought. "Or fake a nervous breakdown."

"And Charles?"

Amelia held her breath for a moment, waiting for the familiar ache at the mention of her husband's name. When it didn't come, she exhaled and considered Ben's question. "He would calmly and rationally explain all the reasons why I shouldn't do it. He would cover everything from money to image to reputation. Then he would squeeze my shoulder and assume the discussion was closed."

"Hmm," Ben said, "the intellectual caveman approach."

Amelia opened her mouth to disagree, then hesitated. She had never thought of Charles as controlling. He'd never lost his temper and had always seemed agreeable. Except when things didn't exactly go his way. She frowned and thought of Ben's blatant, sometimes amusing, bid to get his way. Ben had a temper and could be moody. When he wasn't happy, he laid it on the table. Heaven help her, was she really more at ease with his Conan approach?

Ben must have noticed her shifting on the seat. "Saddle sore?"

"A little," she admitted, eager to think about something else.

"Hungry?"

"Some. Are you?"

"For more than food," he muttered, and buzzed into the parking lot of a small inn with a rowdy eatery that featured barbecued ribs.

The locals were out in force, and since this was the last scheduled stop, most of the bikers were eating. Ben and Amelia grabbed a booth in the back of the large, rustic dining room just as some patrons were leaving.

"I'm beginning to think this was a mistake," he told her, scooting her against the wall and sliding his hands under her coat.

Amelia felt like she'd just been given an injection of pure adrenaline. "Why?"

"Having you wrapped around me for four hours straight, but not being able to make love to you is making me—"

His hands skimmed her breasts and Amelia sucked in a quick breath. "What are you doing?"

Ben groaned and leaned his forehead against hers. "Not as much as I want to do. Not as much as I'm going to do."

His blatant desire for her was deliciously dangerous.

"Ben! Ben Palmer!"

Ben closed his eyes and swore.

"You don't mind sharing your table with us, do you?" a singsong, feminine voice called out.

No sooner had Ben pulled his hands from beneath her sweater, than some of the charity ride participants joined them at the table. Ben reluctantly stood.

The men greeted him with slaps on the back, and the two women gave him enthusiastic hugs. Ben introduced her to the two couples, Frank and Loreen, and Harry and Liz, and the group immediately launched into an intense discussion about motorcycles. Amelia listened and tried to make sense of it, but the terms went straight over her head. Ben's hand on her thigh was the only way she felt connected.

"Frank, I saw you on the side of the road," Ben said. "Problem with the chain again?"

"Yeah, I had to put on a new master link."

"When are you gonna get rid of that chain-eating relic, anyway?" Harry asked after he took a gulp of beer.

"The new belt-driven models give a smoother ride," Ben pointed out.

"It ain't a real Harley if it ain't chain driven," Frank insisted. "Belt-driven Harleys are for sissies."

Loreen looked at Amelia and smiled. "You must be a first timer," she said. "You look lost. Once these guys get started talking transmissions, they don't know how to stop. How long have you known Ben?"

"A couple of months," Amelia said, wondering why it seemed as if she'd known him longer. "Have you participated in other charity runs?"

"A bunch," Loreen said, and gave Amelia an assessing glance. "How long have you been riding motorcycles?"

"I'm just learning," she admitted. "And you?"

"Five years. I'm an officer of the local women riders club, so I'm always on the lookout for new members."

Feeling Liz's curious gaze on her, Amelia smiled, but the other woman didn't return her overture. Amelia struggled with feeling like a fish out of water.

Loreen leaned toward her. "Don't mind Liz," she whispered. "She and Ben went out once, and she wanted to go again, but he didn't."

"Oh," she said, wondering how many other previous girlfriends she was going to trip over. Amelia managed a slight smile. "I'd like to freshen up," she said to Ben.

"Me, too. I'll be back in a minute, you guys," he said and stood with her. "Don't be long, Amelia. The ribs will be out any minute. After we eat," he murmured in a voice for her ears only, "we can get out of here."

His assurance provided a salve to the raw knowledge that she felt like an alien. Amelia pushed open the door to the ladies' room and washed her hands and splashed water on her face. When she looked in the mirror, she couldn't deny who she was. A history professor with wild hair and a cautious mind and nature. She wasn't overly pretty or adventurous or vivacious.

She and Ben were as different as night and day. So why was Ben interested in her? For that matter, why was she interested in him? It was more than interest, her conscience chided, and Amelia exhaled in frustration. Why try to justify something that was neither logical nor rational? Best to just enjoy it, she chanted silently.

Bolstered by her little self-talk, Amelia returned to the table. As she approached, she overheard Liz. "A history professor. She won't hold Ben's attention past Christmas. He'll move on."

Amelia stopped suddenly in the middle of the floor while Liz's words hit her in the face. *He'll move on.* It wasn't anything she hadn't thought before, yet it trickled through her veins like ice water. It was somehow harsher hearing someone else say it.

Ben caught her from behind. "Whoa," he said with a chuckle. "Watch those brakes."

Amelia jerked her head around. "Ben!"

He wrapped his arm around her and lifted his eyebrows. "You were expecting someone else? Who's been hitting on you?"

"No one," she said, tense, and searching his face to see if he'd overheard Liz.

He gently chucked her chin. "You look dazed. C'mon and eat some ribs."

Amelia nodded and gave a small smile. "Sure," she said, wondering how she would swallow a bite.

She managed to get through the meal by moving her food around her plate and nodding and smiling a lot. By the end she felt like one of those novelty dogs with the bobbing heads that sat in the back of cars in the sixties.

"It was nice to meet you," she said as Ben took her by the hand and led her away. Amelia turned toward the entrance. Ben tugged her in the opposite direction. Amelia stumbled after him as he pulled her down the hall into a pantry and closed the door behind them.

Flicking on the light, he leaned against the door and looked at her. "You didn't eat a bite of food… said approximately ten words…and you haven't looked at me for twenty minutes."

Amelia gulped. She'd been so sure he hadn't noticed. "I lost my appetite."

"Why?"

She bit her lip. "I guess I was more tired than I'd thought."

Ben searched her gaze with a power and intensity that shook her, and Amelia had to force herself to remember that he could not read her mind.

He made a tsking sound and slowly moved toward her. "That's bull, darlin'. I want to know what's bothering you, and we can camp out in this pantry until you decide to share." He gave an easy, sexy grin, but his eyes were serious. "Spill it."

Ten

"It was nothing important," Amelia said, and took three steps to one side of the pantry.

Ben studied her carefully. She was fidgety, uneasy. "Did one of the guys hit on you?"

"No," she said quickly. "No."

He frowned. "Then what?"

She sighed and did a minipace to the other side of the pantry. "I overheard something Liz said. It wasn't important."

"Uh-oh," he said, walking closer to her. "This is when the bull starts."

Frustration glinted in her eyes. She tossed him a dark glance. "You're being pushy."

"I can ask nicely," he said dipping his head, though his own patience was stretched. He didn't like seeing Amelia upset. "What did Liz say?"

"I prefer not to talk about it, if you don't mind," she replied.

Ben laced his fingers together and cracked his knuckles. "I mind."

"Oh, *okay!* She said I wouldn't last past Christmas. She said you would move on to someone new."

Ben swore. "Liz lives in a fantasy world and has a big mouth."

"You were involved with her."

"I went out with her once," he corrected.

Amelia groaned. "It doesn't matter," she said, quickly looking away and beginning to pace again. "You and I both know I'm not your usual date—"

"And I'm not yours," he interjected.

"So what she said may very well be true. I know it. You know it. Everyone in the world probably knows it," she said wearily. "It just—" running out of steam, she stopped and shrugged "—it just didn't feel good to hear it."

He hated the lost expression on her face. Ben had a policy about promises and women. He didn't make them. At the moment, though, everything inside him wanted to reassure Amelia. He walked closer to her. "Liz doesn't know what she's talking about."

He lifted her chin, but when she kept her eyes averted, he softly swore. "This is why I don't want to share. I want to keep you and me for you and me. You're different—"

"I know," she said glumly.

"Different in a good way," he told her. "Look at me. I want to see your pretty eyes."

She slowly lifted her gaze to his, and the vulnerability he saw tore at him. "It won't make much sense to anyone else. It may not even make sense to you and me, but we're good for each other.''

Very good, he thought. Amelia made him feel emotions he'd never felt before. He didn't know how she managed it, but she challenged him and soothed him at the same time. If he analyzed it, the way she occupied his mind too many hours of the day could scare the hell out of him.

He shrugged away the thought. ''Besides,'' he told her, ''this is a two-way street. You could leave me under the mistletoe by myself.''

She threw him a skeptical look. ''Talk about bull—''

Sensing the easing of her tension, he pulled her against him. ''Hey, it could happen. You could get bored with me.''

She laughed and shook her head. ''I would *never* get bored with you.''

His gut tightened at the look of desire growing in her eyes. ''Then show me,'' he told her.

She hesitated, then cocked her head to one side. ''*Show* you?''

''Yeah,'' he said, sliding his hands down to her hips. ''Show me.''

She looked at him as if he had lost his mind. ''We're in a pantry.''

''So?''

''Someone can walk through that door any minute.''

He tugged her with him toward the door and leaned his back against it. ''Not now.'' He pulled her between his thighs and watched her eyes widen at his arousal.

"You've got to be kidding," she said, but her voice was husky with excitement.

He shook his head and rotated his pelvis against hers. "Miss Amelia, you sound like you might be a little scared."

She lifted her chin slightly. "I'm not scared. I'm—"

"Chicken," he suggested, and hooked her hands on the pockets of his jeans.

"No," she said.

He lowered his mouth to a millimeter away from hers. "Sissy?"

She leaned forward and brushed her lips against his from side to side, then pulled back. "You don't like sissies?" she asked.

Ben felt his blood heat. "I didn't say that."

She bit her lip, and he swallowed a groan. "Then you *like* sissies?" she asked, sliding her hands down to the front of his jeans.

Ben directed her hands to his belt and zipper. "I *like* you," he said.

She unfastened his pants and took him into her hands.

Burning up from the inside out, he took her mouth while she caressed and stroked him. There was hunger and heat in her touch. She was irresistibly sweet, irrepressibly tempting. The combination was enough to make him crazy.

What had begun as teasing play spiked out of control. He wanted her naked. He wanted to be inside her. All night long. He thrust his tongue past her soft lips, simulating what he wanted to do with his body.

She pulled back slightly, gasping for air, staring at him as she continued to touch him. Her cheeks were flushed with arousal, her eyes dark with passion. Her expression was wild, but tender.

"I—" she began. "I—" She tried again and shook her head as if the words were neither right, nor acceptable.

Then she slid down the front of his body until she rested on her knees. With her gaze still on him, she rubbed her cheek against him, then touched him with her tongue.

When she closed her mouth around him, Ben swore. The sight of her lips taking him was too erotic to bear.

Swollen, too close to the edge, he slid his fingers through her hair. "Sweetheart, stop. I can't—"

Amelia continued making love to him with her mouth, showing him unmistakably how much she wanted him. There was a sensual desperation in her caresses as if, at this moment, giving was the same as receiving.

"Amelia," he protested again, gently urging her away. "Honey, I—"

"Don't make me stop," she whispered, and she took his body and a piece of his heart.

Amelia was so intent on her reading material she didn't hear Sherry enter her office until she stood in front of her desk.

"Hello in there," Sherry said.

Jumping in surprise, Amelia slapped the magazine closed and shoved it onto her lap. "Hi," she said with a smile she hoped was bright enough to blind. "I didn't hear you."

"What were you reading?" she asked in a singsong

voice as she leaned over Amelia's desk. "Did you get another risqué lingerie catalog?"

"Oh, no, nothing like that," Amelia said. "One lingerie catalog was enough. I don't think the leather bra would be at all comfortable."

Sherry tossed her a sly glance. "It must be naughty if you don't want to show me. Come on, let me see."

"It's not naughty," Amelia said, unable to smother a chuckle. "I guarantee it's not naughty."

Sherry held out her hand and wiggled her fingers.

Amelia exhaled, blowing her bangs from her forehead, then reluctantly tossed the magazine onto her desk.

"*Motorcycle Magazine?*" Sherry exclaimed. She gave Amelia a look of mock reproach. "How *low* will you go?"

Amelia thought about what had happened in the pantry and felt her cheeks heat. "Pretty low," she said, swallowing a bad-girl chuckle. "But reading this magazine isn't low. It's a way of educating myself, and there's nothing wrong with education."

Sherry gave a snort of disbelief.

"It's true," she said. "Did you know that not one of the top ten motorcycles-of-the-year is a Harley?"

"You don't say," Sherry said without an ounce of interest. She closed the door. "I realize your brains have taken a temporary walk in the park—or ride on a Harley. But Amelia, you can't be serious about this guy."

Amelia's heart squeezed tight. "I know. You're right," she said. "But I am."

Sherry groaned. "No, no, no, no. You have to stop this. It's the equivalent of the *Titanic. Doomed!*"

She bit her lip. "I think I'm already sunk," she

said in a small voice. "I don't want it to be doomed. I want it to work."

"Oh, Amelia," Sherry said, and shook her head.

"He's good for me," Amelia said. "And I think I might be good for him. Stranger things have happened."

"Not much stranger," Sherry muttered, sitting on the corner of Amelia's desk.

Amelia's hope, however, was growing bigger than her doubt. She laced her fingers together. "I want to see if it can work, if we can work."

"You two are totally different."

"Yes, but that's not necessarily all bad."

"No, but—" Sherry made a face "—you live in two different worlds."

Amelia fought the familiar sinking sensation. "There's no reason we can't visit each other's worlds."

"Have you met any of his friends?"

"Yes," Amelia said, her stomach tightening. "There was a little bit of a language gap. That's part of the reason I got the magazine."

Sherry pinched the bridge of her nose. "They didn't speak English? Amelia, you've got to know this is hopeless."

Amelia stood, rejecting the notion. "It's not hopeless. I know the odds may be stacked against us, but I...I—" She closed her eyes at the power of her feelings for Ben, then blinked back the threat of tears. "He's worth it. He's worth the trouble. He's worth trying for."

Sherry stared at her and sighed. "You sound like you've fallen in love with him."

Amelia clamped her mouth shut. She couldn't say

the words aloud. She was almost afraid that admitting the depth of Ben's effect on her could jinx their future.

"You want to marry him," Sherry said in a stunned voice.

Amelia's stomach took a double dip. She didn't think she would ever want to wrap her life around someone as much as she had with Charles. "Oh, no," she quickly said. "I just thought I'd invite him to the faculty tea."

It was a sunny, unseasonably warm day in early December when Amelia found herself in the middle of a field staring at the motorcycle she was supposed to learn to tame. Painted lime green and much smaller in size than Ben's big, black Harley, the old Suzuki 125 looked more friendly than monstrous.

Fighting nerves, she moved closer and touched the seat. As if petting it might help, she thought wryly.

"Think of it as an unruly bike," Ben told her. "The tricky part is coordination and remembering the gear sequence. Go ahead and hop on."

She resisted the urge to remind him that she would prefer not to kill herself while she was learning. Gingerly, she mounted the bike.

"Here are the basics. You always start in neutral. Let out the clutch with your left hand and let out the throttle with your right hand. You also use your right hand for your front brake."

"Okay," Amelia said with a nod as she worked her hands on the grips and committed his instructions to memory. "I think I can do that."

"That covers your hands."

Disconcerted, she thought this was beginning to

sound like a complicated form of the hokey-pokey. "Oh," she said, glancing up at him and catching his wicked grin. "You're enjoying this a little too much."

He leaned closer to kiss her. "Sweetheart, my enjoyment has just begun," he said, grinning again. "You use your right foot for the rear brake. With your left foot, toe down for first gear, then rock your heel backward and toe up for second gear, then toe up again for third, and toe up again for—"

Her mind muddled, Amelia lifted her hand for him to stop. "I don't think I'll be getting to fourth gear anytime soon. Let's just get me started and moving first."

"Okay, but I need to put this on you," Ben said, proceeding to fasten a Velcro strap around her wrist.

Alarm trickled through her. "Why?"

"It's connected to the kill switch. This way, if you fall off, the bike will turn off instead of dragging you with it."

A disturbing picture of herself being hauled around by a motorcycle gone mad brought second and third thoughts. Amelia looked at Ben again and took a deep breath. She didn't want to show her doubts.

"You start with the kick lever," he said.

Amelia lifted her knee and kicked. Nothing happened.

"Are you in neutral?" he gently asked.

Amelia groaned and moved her left foot into neutral. She kicked the start lever again, and the bike roared to life, vibrating beneath her. She tried to let out the clutch, change gears, and accelerate, but the bike felt as if it ran away from her. It jerked and died. She pitched sideways onto the field.

Ben rushed to her side and helped her up. "You need to work on your clutch action."

Amelia struggled to regain her balance. "I don't suppose any of these come with automatic transmission."

"Aw, those are for siss—"

"Don't start with that sissy stuff," she said heatedly. "I'm in training."

He hesitated, then nodded and kissed her. "You're right," he said, gently touching her cheek. "There's steel underneath all this silk."

Bolstered by his reassurance, Amelia tried again. And again. And again.

The clutch problem was a sore spot because every time she stalled, the bike stopped, and she usually tipped over. Amelia appreciated Ben's calm instructions, and every time she fell, she became a little more determined to tame the lime green monster masquerading as a "fun machine."

Within three hours she could ride for several minutes without causing the engine to stall from her awkward manipulation of the clutch.

Ben called it a day and took her back to his house. She was just about to ask him how she'd done when he said, "I need a drink."

Bemused, she followed after him. "Was I that bad?"

Ben headed straight for the cupboard above the refrigerator in his kitchen and pulled out a bottle of whiskey. He spilled some into a glass and swallowed it in one gulp.

Amelia stared at him. "I couldn't have been that bad," she said. "You were so calm."

"It's important to remain calm during a disaster—"

"Disaster!" Amelia said. "I didn't know I was that bad. Well," she conceded, "I did fall a lot."

"Yep," he said. "I've taught a lot of people to ride a bike, but this was murder on my nerves."

"I was a little scared," she said. "That clutch was the worst."

Ben shook his head and poured another shot of whiskey. "No. The brakes were the worst. Seeing you pitch over the handlebars because you gripped the front brake too much almost made me lose my lunch."

"Next time will be better," Amelia said.

Ben choked on his whiskey. "Next time!"

"Well, yes," she said, watching him. "We knew it would take more than one lesson."

Meeting her gaze, Ben inhaled deeply. "Amelia, I'm not sure I can stomach another lesson."

With her pride taking a beating, she stiffened her spine. "I can't believe I'm the absolute worst rider you've ever taught."

He paused for a long moment. "You're not the worst, but I didn't care much if Billy Stevens broke his leg or got a concussion when he didn't follow my instructions. I don't want you spraining your toenail."

Amelia's heart turned over, and she felt herself become soft and warm inside. She stepped closer and wrapped her arms around him. "I didn't know it was possible to sprain a toenail."

He gave her a mock glare. "Well, don't do it." He dipped his head and took her mouth in a gentle, yet searing kiss. The combination caused an earthquake inside her. When he drew away, the expression on his face almost made her wonder if he felt the same way.

"I think you should take up a different hobby," Ben said.

Still trying to catch her breath, Amelia clung to him. "Like what?"

"Paddleboating," he said.

She blinked. "Paddleboating. That's tough to do in the winter."

"Okay, how about something where you can stay warm like—" he hesitated a half beat "—like knitting."

Amelia gaped at him, then shook her head. "Wait a minute. You've been telling me I'm a sissy because I haven't gambled or trespassed or driven a motorcycle."

"It's okay for a woman to be a sissy."

She laughed and pulled away from him. "Ben Palmer, that is the most sexist remark I've ever heard you say, and you've said some whoppers. I'm going to learn to drive a motorcycle."

He snagged her wrist, his face serious. "I don't want you to get hurt."

The intensity in his voice chipped away at her meager defenses against him. She would never have dreamed he would care this much for her. "I don't want to get hurt, either, but I can't live my life missing out on doing things I want to do because I'm afraid. You wouldn't want to live your life that way, either."

Clearly torn, Ben sighed. "It's different with you. You're important, too important. I couldn't watch you get hurt."

Amelia felt herself slipping. He could make her

want him for a long time, especially if he kept talking this way, if he kept looking at her this way. "You're important to me, too." She turned her hand over to lace her fingers through his. "Should I find someone else to teach me to drive? I think there are classes—"

"Hell, no!" He frowned. "If anyone is going to teach you, it'll be me."

Her lips twitched at the passion in his voice. "It might take nerves of steel to get me ready for the road. Are you sure you want to do it?"

He glowered at her. "It'll take something else made of steel, so it's a damn good thing I've been told I've got those, too."

Amelia remembered the plan she'd kept to herself and took a deep breath. It was time to broach it with Ben. The moment was now. Part of her held back. After all, she'd performed her scary thing for the day. Amelia was certain what she was about to do was far more scary than learning to drive a motorcycle.

"Well, if you truly have steel—" she referred to his comment and tried for a confident smile "—*nerves,* then I'd like you to do something else with me next weekend."

He gave her a curious glance. "What's that?"

"Go with me to the faculty tea," she said, and knew she'd just made a dare that could turn their private world upside down.

Eleven

Ben stared at her silently for a long, nerve-shattering moment until Amelia thought she would scream from the tension. This was an important step for them.

With a dead-serious expression, he lifted his hand to her forehead. "Why didn't you tell me you got a concussion when you fell?"

She swatted his hand away. "Oh-h-h-h, stop! I'm serious. I want you to join me for the faculty Christmas tea."

Ben shook his head. "Me in a room full of stuffy professor types listening to chamber music and eating liver and fish eggs on crackers."

"I'm not stuffy," she said, disputing one of his points.

"True," he conceded. "But you usually conceal your wild side from society. I don't. I'm not the right kind of guy for this job."

"Are you saying I should take another man?"

"No," he said immediately, then downed the last remnants of his scotch. Sighing, he met her gaze and brushed his fingertips over her lips. "Miss Amelia, we've already talked about this. When it's just you and me, it's great. But when we start letting in the outside world, it doesn't work so well. Everything's terrific in private. Going public won't work for us."

She lifted her hand to press his hand against her mouth. "We went public for the charity motorcycle ride," she pointed out.

"Yep, and somebody shot off her mouth, and you got your feelings hurt," he reminded her, and pulled her into his embrace. "Haven't you heard the expression 'if it ain't broke, don't fix it'?"

Amelia's heart tightened. "Of course I've heard it, but I'm proud of you, Ben. I think you're the most incredible man in the world. You're smart and interesting and generous. Yes, you're a little wild, but you're terrific," she said, smiling despite her strong emotions. She wrapped her arms around him. "I want everyone I know to get a chance to meet you."

He looked at her with a mixture of bemusement and pleasure. "Aw, Amelia—" He broke off and shook his head.

"What?" she asked.

He swore. "I don't believe this. You scare the stuffing out of me, trying to ride that damn bike, then—" He swore again. "No one's ever said anything like that to me," he scolded, fiddling with her hair.

"Anything like what?" she gently prodded, charmed by his self-conscious gratification.

He squinted his eyes and shrugged. "No one's ever said they were proud of me."

Surprised, she felt her stomach sink. "Sure they have," she said. "Your parents—"

"Nope." He shook his head. "It's no big deal, but I wasn't exactly an easy kid," he said wryly.

Amelia saw the hole in his life, the need that had never been filled, and it hurt her. "Come with me to the faculty tea. Go public," she urged.

The light in his eyes dimmed, and she felt a sad sense of foreboding. "I can't do that. We're better alone," he told her, and kissed her. "Let me show you how good we are alone."

That night he made love to her tenderly, beautifully. He kissed her boo-boos from her riding lesson and whispered his praise of her body. He told her she made him crazy and seduced her with his words and his body. Amelia had never experienced such passion. He made her feel alive. He took her to the top again and again. If she didn't know better, his eyes said, "I love you, I love you, I love you...."

Just for tonight she pretended she didn't know better.

Replete and satisfied in nearly every possible way, Amelia snuggled in his arms. She couldn't dispute him. He was right. Behind closed doors, they were perfect.

When Ben awakened the next morning, he instinctively reached for Amelia, but his hands encountered cool sheets instead. He rubbed his eyes with the back of his hand and lifted his head to look for her.

His heart picked up at his first sight of her. Dressed in the clothes she'd worn yesterday, she stood facing the window with her arms wrapped around her waist as if she were hugging herself.

A dozen emotions hit him at once. Somehow she had become more to him than he'd expected. Somehow she had become more to him than anyone ever had. She brought him a peace he'd never experienced. Conversely, that disturbed the hell out of him.

"Up with the sunshine this morning?" he asked, rising from the bed and pulling on his jeans.

She turned her head and smiled, but she had a faraway look in her eyes. "I heard Caesar yelling for his cat food."

He strolled to her and skimmed his hand down her arm to bring all her attention back to him. With each day, Ben found himself growing increasingly greedy for Amelia. "Are you telling me that cat is a rival against me for your affections?"

She gave him a sideways glance. "'That cat,' which *you* gave me thinks he rules the house."

"And does he?"

"Sometimes, but on the important issues I rule."

"Name an important issue," Ben said, wishing she didn't seem so distant.

"He's getting neutered this week," she said with a grin.

Ben winced. "Ouch. I'd definitely say you rule."

Amelia brushed her hand over his bare shoulder, then met his gaze with that distracted expression again. "I need to go."

He nodded, but he was confused by the unsettled feeling in his gut. "Let me get my—"

"But I want you to come with me to the faculty tea," she said.

"I thought we settled that," Ben said, frowning. "We're better off not getting involved with each other's outside worlds."

"No. We discussed it, but it's not settled. I still feel the same way. I want everyone I know to get a chance to meet you." She hesitated and took a careful breath as if she were searching for courage. "I'm in love with you," she said, looking him straight in the eye.

Her words hit him like an arrow from a crossbow. Reeling, he nearly stumbled backward. He had never known such intense joy and fear inside the same moment. He blew out a puff of air. "I, uh—"

She shook her head. "You don't have to say anything. I just had to tell you," she said with a shrug and a smile, but the upturn of her lips looked a little strained. "I was going to burst if I didn't."

She drew away, a look of concentration on her face. "These feelings I have for you are big. They stretch me on the inside and the outside. The kind of man you are pushes me to grow, to step outside myself. Hiding the way I feel about you isn't going to work. Confining our relationship to your house or mine isn't going to be enough. I want to know you as much as you'll let me, and I want you to know me. It's scary because our worlds are so different, but knowing you is helping me to be a little less fearful."

Ben ran his hand through his hair and began to pace. He was still knocked off his feet by her declaration. He knew Amelia wasn't the kind to say those words lightly. He'd heard them from other women and felt burdened. This time was different. He swore and stopped directly in front of her. "I don't want to lose what we have because of some stupid opinion our families, friends or colleagues might have."

"Who says we have to lose?" she asked, smiling as if she were trying to lighten the heavy tone.

But Ben had a deep foreboding of disaster. He felt as if he was a runaway train about to run out of track.

The Christmas tree in the Salem College tearoom was decorated with vintage, colorful, glass ornaments and sparkling white lights. The serving table was dressed in red-and-white linen with poinsettias in full bloom. Piped-in stringed holiday music provided an elegant aural atmosphere.

But all Amelia could hear in the background of her mind was Elvis Presley's rendition of "Blue Christmas."

He's not coming. Amelia looked at the door for the hundredth time in fifteen minutes.

"He's not coming," Sherry said.

"He might," Amelia said, fighting her own doubt and trying to keep the note of defensiveness out of her voice. She had hoped. Oh, how she had hoped.

"He's not coming," Sherry repeated. "But you look killer in that suit. Where'd you get it?"

"Thanks. I found it in a mail-order catalog," she said, and absently returned a wave to the dean as she checked the door once more.

"Stop watching," Sherry said, urging her toward the table loaded with appetizers. "Mingle. Eat something. Let me introduce you to—omigod—"

Amelia spun around to look at the doorway.

"Sheesh, Amelia, are you trying to get whiplash?" Sherry asked. "Would you close your mouth? If you light up anymore, you'll look like a Christmas tree..."

Amelia didn't hear anything else Sherry said. She just saw Ben, and her heart beat double time. He stood in the doorway, wearing his leather jacket, minus the earring. Elvis's "Blue Christmas" faded away, and Handel's "Hallelujah Chorus" took its place in her mind.

He came!

She squinted. What kind of tie was he wearing?

He looked uncomfortable enough to turn around and leave. Amelia moved quickly toward him.

She smiled. "You came!"

He nodded, looking around the room. "I came."

Her smile grew wider at the complete lack of enthusiasm in his voice. She hooked her hand through his arm. "Good news," she said. "There are meatballs."

He glanced at some of the other professors. "I can see that."

She laughed. "C'mon. I'll introduce you around."

Moving with her, he snagged a glass of wine. "Lead the way."

"Just out of curiosity," she ventured, heading for Sherry, "where's your earring?"

"Pocket," he said.

"Ben, this is Sherry Kiggins. She took me to the Thunderbird Club."

"Nice to meet you," he said. "I owe you."

She gave him a considering glance and nodded. "Yes, you do. Amelia's a rare gem, but I'm sure you know that. I like your tie," she added. " 'Roadrunner' is one of my favorite cartoons. With a stocking hat, he's right in season."

"I'll pass your compliments on to my nephew. He gave me this for Christmas last year. And you're right about Amelia," he added.

Embarrassed by the compliment, Amelia felt her cheeks heat. "Enough about gems."

"The slit in your skirt is a tease," he said into Amelia's ear as she waved at Sherry and led him away. "Take me home, take off your clothes and put me out of my misery."

Her heart turned over. "Stop tempting me. I'm still pinching myself that you're here."

"Is that a yes?"

"Maybe."

"Now?"

"Later," she said firmly. "Oh, here comes Dr. Allbright." She saw the portly man walking toward them. "He's a calculus professor, and the head of the math department."

After they were introduced, Ben grinned and shook his hand. "I gotta tell you I flunked high school algebra."

Dr. Allbright nodded. "You probably thought you had better things to do in high school than algebra."

Ben chuckled. "Probably. I always thought those formulas were secretly designed to make your brain explode."

Dr. Allbright's lips twitched. "And now?"

"Now it's still simple arithmetic, not algebra. I own and manage a foreign car dealership."

Dr. Allbright raised his eyebrows. "You don't say. I just heard the dean talking about a Mercedes he might want to buy."

Ben cocked his head to one side consideringly. "You need to be careful. Some of them are great, but there's one model that rides like a roller skate. You ride over a dime, and you can tell if it's heads or tails."

"Is that so?" He gestured to the dean and waved

him over. "Dean Ericson, we've got an automobile expert here."

Soon Amelia and Ben were surrounded by several members of the faculty. He spent the next hour giving car consultations. Amelia had hoped he would be received well, but even she was surprised by the way her peers responded to him. It was almost as if they were relieved to discuss something other than academics.

As she and Ben prepared to leave, Dean Ericson tapped her on the shoulder. "Interesting guest you brought us, Amelia."

She smiled. "Thank you. I think so, too."

The dean chuckled. "I can't wait to see who you bring next time," he said, then left.

Amelia stared after him in confusion. As she drove home, however, the light dawned, and she frowned. The dean thought Ben was a novelty item, and perhaps she would trade him in for a different novelty. The notion made her want to kick something.

"Stuffy old goat," she muttered as Ben joined her on her front porch and they walked through her doorway.

"Excuse me?" Ben said.

"Nothing," she murmured. "What can I get you to drink?"

"You've got your panties in a twist about the dean," Ben said, catching her hand and pulling her over to the sofa. "I told you—"

"Don't you dare say 'I told you so.' For the most part, the evening went much better than I hoped, let alone what you hoped."

Ben nodded and pulled her down on his lap. "Uh-huh," he said in a noncommittal tone.

"They loved you," Amelia said.

Ben shot her a look of disbelief. "That's a slight exaggeration."

"Well, they liked you."

He rested his forehead against hers. "Don't beat your head against the wall, sweetheart. They didn't see us as a likely pair."

She thought about what he'd said for a long moment. She wanted everyone to know how terrific Ben was. She wanted everyone to see they were good together, but what Ben thought was far more important to her. "What do you see, Ben?"

He touched her cheek. "I see a beautiful woman, inside and out." He slid his other hand down her hip and over her thigh. "I see a beautiful suit that's going to be history in a few minutes." He paused, and his expression grew serious. "I see a dangerous woman."

Surprised and moved, she felt a lump of emotion form in her throat. "I'm not dangerous."

"You are to me."

"Ben was a December baby," Maddie told Amelia on the phone. "Poor guy. He usually doesn't get much of a birthday celebration. With my parents taking a Christmas cruise this year, I thought I'd fix dinner for him at my house the day before Christmas Eve. Can you join us?"

Amelia remembered Ben's reluctance for them to share each other's worlds and felt a double pinch of pain. "I'd love to come, but—" She twisted the phone cord, uncertain what to say.

"Are you busy?"

"No, but—"

"Well, are you two still seeing each other?"

"Yes, but—"

"Then you can come," Maddie said cheerfully.

Struggling with frustration and her desire to respect Ben's wishes, she sighed. "I'm not sure if Ben would prefer to keep it just family, and since it's his birthday—"

Maddie groaned. "He's never acted this weird before. Sure he's always been Mr. Privacy about his love life, but with you it's like he's the secret service and you're the president. Would you like to join us if I clear it with him?"

"Of course—"

"Then I'll tell him I've invited you," she said decisively. "That'll be the day before Christmas Eve at noon. See ya!"

Amelia tried to reply, but found herself speaking to a dead line. She slowly hung up the phone and sank down into a chair. Caesar jumped on her lap and regally lifted his head for her to rub him. Her lips twitched. For a tomcat, he sure thought he was something special.

For a human tomcat, Ben Palmer sure was something special, she thought. With each passing day, she wanted to be with him more and more. It was crazy, but she even hated saying goodbye to him at night when he went home. She wondered if he felt the same way. Since the charity motorcycle ride, he hadn't uttered the word *temporary*.

Amelia had never felt this strongly for her husband. That knowledge sometimes made her feel guilty. After all, she and Charles had made lifetime promises to each other.

The past year, however, had changed her in ways that permeated her appearance, her home, even her profession. She smiled when she thought of the recent assignment she'd given her class in American history. Her students were to write an essay on a woman who had made an important contribution to the American colonies. Some of the guys had groaned, but she'd been pleased with the opportunity to pry open their minds. She'd been even more pleased with the results.

Before Amelia had often done everything by the book. It had been safer. Gradually she was learning to develop and enjoy her own creativity.

With Ben she felt more alive and happy with herself than she ever had. He made life an adventure. He challenged her. He brought her oranges and encouraged her to grow.

Her thoughts should have made her smile, but Amelia felt an undercurrent of something that smelled and tasted like fear inside her. It was the niggling feeling of something not quite right that surfaced every now and then. It was more than the fact that Ben had never said aloud that he loved her. He'd shown love to her in many ways.

She didn't need reassuring words from him to know that what she shared with Ben was special, she told herself, did she? She also told herself that she wasn't so conventional that she needed marriage. Surely she was more broad-minded than that.

Wasn't she?

Twelve

At the front door of the main house of their beautiful horse ranch, Maddie, her husband, Joshua, and Davey greeted Amelia and Ben.

"Happy birthday, Uncle Ben!" Davey yelled as he wrapped himself around Ben's legs. "Mom said you're thirty. You're *old!*"

Amelia laughed at the disconcerted expression on Ben's face. "Next thing you know, he'll be after your Harley."

"Oh, no," a young man just inside the door said. "I've got dibs on his Harley. Happy birthday, old man."

"Old man. You'll be lucky to get a motor scooter from me." Ben gave the younger man a bear hug, then turned to Amelia. "This is Joshua's son, Patrick, home from college."

"He's *mine*, too," Maddie insisted.

Patrick nodded. "As long as she's cooking, I'm all hers."

"My son is still ruled by his gut," Joshua said in mock disgust.

The group exchanged friendly greetings, and it took some explanations, but Amelia finally learned that Joshua had married Maddie a few years ago after she had given birth to Davey. In fact, a crazy coincidence had enabled him to help deliver Davey. From the easy affection they all showed each other, one would never know they weren't all blood relatives.

They quickly embraced Amelia with a warm curiosity and humor that made her feel like a necessary part of this special occasion. Never far from her side, Ben touched the back of her waist or at times took her hand. His proximity served as a constant reminder to her of how much her feelings for him continued to grow stronger. If she wasn't careful, she could wish for more, far more than he would want to give.

Dinner was a man's meal, prime rib with roasted potatoes, deliciously prepared. Amelia complimented Maddie and received a quick hug in response.

"Time for the cake," Maddie said, bringing the chocolate, layered dessert lit with thirty candles to the table. "I wasn't going to put this many candles on it, but Davey insisted. I put the fire department on alert," she added slyly, "just in case."

After a slightly off-key chorus of "Happy Birthday," Ben was urged to make a wish and blow out the candles.

"Before the house burns down," Joshua cryptically said.

"Speaking of age," Ben retorted meaningfully.

"Be nice," Maddie said with an innocent grin. "Joshua can't help it he's old."

Joshua playfully swatted Maddie on the rear and pulled her onto his lap. "The candles," he said to Ben.

Ben gave a self-conscious shrug. He closed his eyes for a moment, then extinguished the candles.

Amelia would have traded a year of good-hair days to know what he'd wished. She would have traded her house to be a permanent part of his life, to have a permanent place in his heart. Her chest squeezed tight at the way her own buried wishes popped to the surface.

Ben leaned over and quickly kissed her, and she felt a shocking threat of tears.

Concern deepened his brown eyes. "What's wrong?" he asked in a low voice.

She blinked quickly and smiled, shaking her head. "Nothing. I'm just glad I'm here."

"I am, too," he said.

And she held her breath at the look in his gaze. She could almost believe… Almost.

After the cake was demolished, Maddie herded everyone into the living room. "In honor of the fact that my brother has survived yet another year, and the fact that I have survived being his sister despite his reckless, daredevil, insane, deadly stubborn—"

Joshua cleared his throat loudly. "We got the picture, Maddie."

"Oh," Maddie said and chuckled. She turned on the television. "For your viewing pleasure, 'The Life and Times of Ben Palmer.'"

The first picture that came into focus featured a little girl, Maddie, holding her baby brother Ben on her lap. It was a Kodak moment until Ben started howling and Maddie plugged her fingers in her ears.

Ben groaned. "Where did you find this?"

"Mom and Dad gave me full access to all those videos they took when we were little."

"Great," he muttered. "Sorry to put you through this," he said to Amelia. "I didn't know Maddie had planned a movie of me."

Amelia squeezed his hand. "Oh, I want to see it. This is better than an old photo album."

Ben made a gruff sound of disbelief, but laced his fingers through hers.

The next shot showed baby Ben chewing on a plastic toy car. Then he was roaring over the patio in a walker.

"From the very beginning," Maddie said. "He liked everything that had wheels. He started his hair-raising stunts at an early age by flying down the steps in the walker. Mom nearly had a breakdown, but Ben was smiling."

Amelia drank in the images of Ben transforming from tyke to a little boy racing his big wheel, then moving on to a bicycle.

"Your knees were always scuffed," she said to Ben.

He nodded wryly. "Yeah. I was rough on my elbows, too."

"There are no movies with you with training wheels."

"That's right. I thought training wheels were for—"

"Sissies," she finished for him and rolled her eyes. "Why am I not surprised?"

The impression of Ben as a child branded her mind

and heart. She wondered if his son or daughter would look like him, if his son or daughter would be hell-on-wheels. For a second, Amelia allowed herself to feel the depth of her longing to be the woman to give him that child. Her yearning seemed bottomless, and she took a deep breath to ease the ache.

Another scene crossed the screen of a ragtag group of boys in front of a tree house.

"The Bad Boys Club," Ben said with a nostalgic grin.

Amelia was filled with more wishes. She wished she'd known him them. She wished she could know him the rest of her life.

"The terrors of Cherry Lane," Maddie said.

Amelia studied the scene of Ben and his friends. It was clear that all of the boys were trying to look tough. No smiles allowed until Ben started a water balloon fight.

Soon the pictures showed Ben as a teen on a motorbike, then his first motorcycle. He looked so daring and so proud that her heart twisted again.

The scene shifted again. This time, a girl with long, blond hair joined Ben on his motorcycle.

"Ah, now we have the women," Maddie said in a teasing voice. "Can you name that girl?"

Ben scrunched up his face. "Debbie?"

"Gail," Maddie said.

Another scene and another girl. "Who is this one?" Maddie prompted.

"Lisa?"

Maddie snickered. "Kara."

Ben rubbed his forehead. "You didn't do all of them, did you?"

"I didn't have time for an epic," Maddie said.

"You've slowed down during the past few years. But we might have to drug you or hit you over the head to get you down the aisle."

"There she goes again," Ben said to Amelia. "Now that Maddie is happily married, she can't stand the idea that other people can be happily single."

He chuckled and seemed to be waiting for Amelia to say something, but she couldn't form the words. The lump in her throat prevented her.

Feeling his inquisitive gaze, Amelia panicked. She hoped he couldn't read her thoughts from her face. She quickly glanced at the TV and pointed at the new scene of Ben kicking up dust while he drove an obstacle course. "What's that?" she managed.

He turned back to the television, and Amelia sighed with relief.

"That was one of the competitions I entered to meet the requirements for Class B Trials Enduro Rider."

Amelia cringed at the sharp turns he took. The bike bowed low to the ground. "How did you keep from wrecking?"

He lifted his hand. "Watch."

A second later he wiped out on a hairpin turn and his bike went careening down a hill. Amelia's heart stopped. "Omigod! You did that on purpose!"

He grinned and nodded. "Yep, and it wasn't the only time."

"Did you have to go to the hospital?"

"Not that time."

The bike finally stopped, and while Ben got off and dusted himself off, a woman ran toward him and threw her arms around him.

Ben lifted his hand and covered her eyes. "I think you've seen enough."

Amelia wedged his fingers apart, but the scene had changed. Watching the next episodes of Ben performing increasingly dangerous motorcycle stunts made her stomach clench. A couple of times she had to look away. She had known he was a risk taker, but she'd had no idea how far he had gone. It was a wonder he hadn't been killed doing the stunts. She wondered what had driven him to take such risks. She wondered if he'd gotten it out of his system.

Ben watched himself at a younger, more reckless, age as he whizzed down a dirt obstacle course. He felt Amelia's fingernails dig into his hand. "Problem?" he asked.

She shook her head. "No," she said in a high-pitched voice.

"Then why are you shredding my hand?"

She jerked her gaze down to her tense fingers and pulled her hand from his. "Oops. Sorry."

Her concern warmed him, even though the moment for fear had long since passed. She had a tender heart for a woman with so much spirit. He put his arm around her stiff shoulders. "The video makes it look worse than it was."

He watched her flinch at another wipeout. "Uh-huh," she said without an ounce of conviction.

He felt her breathe a sigh of relief when the final installment showed him dressed as Santa buzzing into the youth center with a red sack on his Harley.

Everyone applauded at the end, and Davey immediately thrust a gift in his lap. "Open it," he insisted.

He hugged his nephew for the giant bag of candy.

After opening the gifts from the rest of his family, Amelia gave him a small box.

Curious, he shook it, but didn't hear a rattle. "What is it?"

She smiled. "You have to open it to find out."

"Animal, vegetable or mineral?" he asked.

"Vegetable," she said. "Although some would say animal. Many women would say animal," she added wryly.

He did a double take. "A guy gift."

Still smiling, she shrugged. "Could be."

He opened the package and gaped at the two small slips of paper he found inside. "Tickets to a Bulls' game?"

"The *Bulls!*" Joshua and Patrick yelled at the same time. They nearly stampeded each other to get close to Ben.

"Is this a joke?" Ben asked Amelia.

She looked offended. "Of course not."

"You've got two tickets," Patrick said. "I can go with you."

"Pipe down, junior," Joshua said. "I'll go."

For a moment Ben wondered if father and son would draw blood.

Maddie cleared her throat. "It's Ben's birthday present, you guys, so don't you think he should decide who goes with him?"

For once Ben was grateful for his sister's assertive nature. "Thanks, Maddie."

Joshua and Patrick grumbled, but it was time for Davey to hit the sack, and Ben seized the opportunity to leave.

At the door Joshua thumped Ben on the back. "Are you still thinking about the offer you've received for the dealership? Are you really going to turn over the reins and take a cross-country trek on your bike?''

Ben felt Amelia's gaze and shrugged. ''I don't know. My buyer upped his offer, and he wants an answer by next week.''

Maddie stared at him. ''You wouldn't really sell the dealership, would you?''

''I haven't decided,'' Ben said. ''I never planned to be the boss, and there are a ton of headaches that come with the job. This kind of offer doesn't come along every day.''

''But—'' Maddie said.

''He's a grown-up.'' Joshua put his arm around her. ''Ben'll make the right decision for himself.''

Ben noticed his sister's worried expression, but they said goodbye and rode away in Amelia's car. Since the temperature was close to freezing, Amelia had persuaded Ben to allow her to chauffeur him.

Amelia was quiet, he thought, after she hadn't said a word for ten minutes. Too quiet.

''How'd you get the Bulls tickets?'' he asked.

She didn't answer.

''Amelia,'' he prompted, gently squeezing her shoulder.

She blinked. ''Oh, I'm sorry. I didn't hear you.''

''The Bulls tickets, how'd you get them?''

She gave a slight smile. ''It was partly payback. I was drafted to tutor the basketball team, so I asked the coach for gift ideas. He gave me some phone numbers, and I went from there. I didn't know I would cause a reenactment of the Civil War in your family.''

Ben chuckled at the distress in her voice. ''They're just sick with jealousy. They wish they had a woman in their lives clever enough to get them such a great gift.''

"I don't think Joshua would want to trade in Maddie for Bulls tickets," Amelia said.

"Maybe not," he said, and chuckled at her shocked glance. He squeezed her shoulder again. "What's with you tonight? You seem tense."

She pulled to a stop at a traffic light. "The video was riveting, but it was difficult to watch you doing some of those dangerous stunts and hurting yourself." She shuddered. "You told me you were more reckless when you were younger, but you've always been so safe when I've been with you that I guess it didn't quite compute."

"That's all history," he assured her.

"Is it?" she asked, her voice growing tighter. "Do you ever get a yen to bounce your bike off logs on an obstacle course?"

"Not for a while," he told her, then leaned closer and teased, "You're not really afraid I'm gonna kill myself, are you?"

Amelia stiffened. "It's not a joke! I couldn't bear it if you hurt yourself. I—" She broke off and took a deep breath. "Not that I have any rights where you're concerned. I realize we're in a—" she pursed her lips and seemed to force the word out "—temporary relationship. But I care for you and would never ever want to see you hurt."

The way she said *temporary* jangled his nerves, but he was more concerned about comforting her. "I'm very careful now. You don't need to worry, sweetheart."

She gave a noncommittal nod and made the turn into her neighborhood. She said nothing for several moments, and the silence stretched between them. Ben sensed the turmoil in her.

"Did the women in the movie Maddie made bother you?"

She gave a tiny wince. "Not as much as the wrecks. There was definitely a different girl for every season, though," she said quietly.

"Most of that was shot a long time ago," he told her, thinking it might have been best if Amelia had never seen that movie. He liked the fact that she knew him for the man he was now, instead of the angry youth he used to be.

She pulled into her drive and stopped the car. Keeping her gaze forward, she bit her lip. "So, are you serious about selling the dealership?"

Her calm voice was at odds with the tension she emanated. Ben answered honestly. "It's a good offer. I would be a fool not to consider it."

"What will you do if you sell?"

Reluctant to admit one of his longtime dreams, he hesitated, then shrugged. "I always thought I'd like to ride across country on my bike. No hotel reservations, no time restraints, just follow the road."

She smiled, but it didn't quite come off as a happy curve to her lips. "I can see how you would like that. Have you thought about what you would do after the trip?"

"Not really," Ben confessed. "I might find a different place I'd want to live for a while. Anything could happen. I think that's what I like about the idea. Every day would be new, and I wouldn't feel stuck in a rut."

She turned to look at him and cocked her head to one side. "Do you feel stuck in a rut now?"

"I have," he said. "Not as much lately, but…" He frowned, trying to put his finger on when that sense of being in a rut had faded. "My buyer wants an answer by the end of the year, so I'll decide this week."

"You've got a lot to think about."

"Yeah," he said, wondering what was going on in Amelia's mind. He could touch her, yet she seemed distant. He lifted his hand to the back of her head. "But right now I'm thinking about you. Did my sister's family scare you off?"

"Of course not. They're so warm and loving. You're lucky," she told him, solemnly meeting his gaze. "They're pretty lucky, too."

His heart swelled in his chest, and he pulled her as close as he could with the console between them. "Oh, Amelia, only you would say that."

"That's not true. Davey would," she said. "Maddie might."

He looked into her soft eyes and felt the jagged need for her in the secret places of his heart that he kept locked and protected. He wanted her with his mind. He wanted her with his body. The force of his desire for her infiltrated dark needs he'd revealed to no one. She loved him and could make him feel it with a few words or a simple touch. He trusted her as if she were his own flesh.

The realization rumbled through him, shaking him.

He took her mouth and wanted her soul. He'd never known a man could want a woman this much. He kissed her until they couldn't breathe.

He pulled back and sucked in a breath of air. "I could take you right now in the front seat of your car."

Her hand trembled as she brushed her hair from her face. "And I'd probably let you," she whispered, then closed her eyes for a moment as if she were searching for her sense. "I can't invite you to stay all night tonight. My mother's flight arrives early in the morning."

"That's okay," he said, even though he didn't want to leave her tonight. He didn't feel reasonable about Amelia at the moment. Although he loved his sister and her family, he wished he'd kept Amelia to himself this evening. "But let me walk you to the door before I change my mind."

The cool air hit his face like a slap of aftershave in the morning. There was something bothering Amelia. He couldn't nail it, but she seemed distracted. "How long is your mom staying?"

"Five days," she said as she joined him on the front porch.

Vaguely bummed, he nodded. "Dinner after she leaves?"

She hesitated a beat. "I look forward to it. You're still coming tomorrow night for dinner, aren't you?"

"I wouldn't miss it." He gave a wry grin, thinking about all the mothers he'd met and horrified. "Are you sure this is a good idea? I tend to make mothers nervous."

She set her chin. "I'm sure it's a good idea. I want my mother to meet you."

Skeptical, he leaned closer and kissed her. "Okay."

When she pulled back, she met his gaze wholeheartedly. "Happy birthday, Ben. The world is a better place because of you. I'm so very glad you were born."

The words were indescribably tender, as was the touch of her hand on his cheek. It wasn't until he drove home, however, that it struck Ben that the expression in her eyes looked much too sad.

Thirteen

───

She was a Southern lady with a capital *L*. Silver
white hair, magnolia skin with a few expression lines
that revealed her maturity, eyes that sparkled with
warmth and intelligence, and a Southern accent that
brought to mind the long, slow kick of bourbon in a
mint julep.

"I understand you've been teaching Amelia to ride
a motorcycle," she said to Ben as they sat at the
dining room table for the holiday meal. Amelia had
pulled out the stops with delicious food, fine china
and delicate crystal. "How is she doing?"

"I almost quit after the first lesson," Ben admitted.
"But your daughter is no quitter."

Grace smiled. "Amelia has always struggled to
conquer anything connected with the invention of the
wheel. My husband, God bless him, always said most

of his hair turned gray when he was teaching her to ride a bicycle.''

"I've had three lessons, and Ben says I'm just about ready for the road," Amelia said.

Grace sighed. "Oh, my goodness, if I had any hair that wasn't gray, you would turn it. Why in the world would you want to drive a motorcycle?"

Amelia topped off her mother's wineglass and tossed Ben a secret glance of amusement. "It's fun."

Grace fussed over the danger of motorcycles for a few more minutes before giving up, then she turned her attention back to Ben. He was conversationally, but persistently questioned about everything from his job to his eating habits to his educational background. He had to hand it to her. Grace made the inquisition go down fairly easy with smiles and a few stories about Amelia. He didn't need a brain like Einstein's to understand that she was checking his suitability for her daughter.

Ben noticed her daughter grew more tense throughout the meal. Constantly aware of her, he tried to read her mood. There was an unsettled air about her, as if she were struggling with something and it was making her unhappy. Ben found himself wanting to settle the unsettled. It was important to him for Amelia to be happy, and it frustrated the hell out of him that he wouldn't be alone with her until her mother left town.

When Amelia excused herself to the kitchen to slice the pecan pie, Grace gazed at Ben with sincerity. "When Charles died, it was very hard on Amelia. So many dreams for her were lost in that instant. I wanted to protect her, but she must have known she needed to grow into her own woman. That was why she took the position at Salem College and moved here." Grace patted his hand. "You've helped my daughter smile again. For that, I'll always be grateful."

Amelia appeared in the doorway with three plates of pie. "Mother, are you flirting again?"

Ben watched color rise in Grace's cheeks and squeezed the genteel woman's hand. "Yes. You better come and rescue me. I'm completely under her spell," Ben said, and both women laughed.

After a few minutes he noticed Amelia was distracted. "Problem?" he asked her.

"I checked downstairs, and I think Caesar is missing," she said with a frown of concern. "I'm keeping him in the basement while Mother visits, but he likes to wander. It's cold tonight. If you two will excuse me, I'd better go outside and look for him."

"I'll do it," he said, rising, needing a breath of air. Although he enjoyed Grace's warmth, Ben had never long endured being the subject of study beneath a magnifying glass. Her questions had unleashed an uneasiness inside him.

It was a cold, star-filled night, and walking around the perimeter of Amelia's yard, Ben felt as if the differences between him and Amelia were drawn in bold, black ink. He couldn't care less what other people thought, because he knew she was the best thing that had happened to him. His concern, however, was that Amelia wouldn't always be able to stand against the naysayers. She was more sensitive than he was, and she'd clearly been raised to follow social conventions.

Ben inhaled the bitter cold air and shoved the gut-twisting thoughts from his head. He had to find a tomcat. After searching the yard several times, he found the scalawag in the bushes next to the porch. He carried the escapee back into the house and overheard Amelia and her mother talking in the kitchen.

"He seems very nice, but he's not at all like Charles," Grace said.

"Ben is very independent. I admire that about him," Amelia said, her taut voice joining the clatter of dishes.

"Amelia, I'm sure I don't have to tell you that there are men for fun and there are men for marriage. Ben may be kind, but he's not marriage material. Don't you want to get married again?"

A long silence followed. "I don't know if I'll get married again," Amelia finally said. "I know Ben isn't marriage material. I know he won't ever want to commit himself to me. The day may come when that will hurt me too much to continue with him," she said, and the sadness in her voice told Ben that day could come sooner than he might want.

"But now, I'm just glad I know him. He's a very special man."

Caesar let out a loud yowl and clawed Ben's hand. He swore, immediately dropping the tomcat.

Amelia and Grace rushed into the den.

"I brought your ungrateful cat inside," Ben said with a scowl as he rubbed the scratch mark.

Amelia's lips twitched. "You keep forgetting that *you* gave him to me."

"Maybe I should have let him freeze."

She looked at his hand. "Thank you for bringing him in. Let me fix your scratch."

Drinking in the last few moments of their time together, he allowed Amelia to fuss over the scratch mark. A few minutes later Ben wished Grace a happy

Christmas, then bundled up Amelia and dragged her outside with him. He pulled her close and kissed her. "Are you sure she isn't with the CIA?"

Amelia laughed breathlessly. "They took lessons from her. I just hope she didn't bore you with those stories about me as a child."

"No chance," he told her, drinking in her scent and memorizing how she felt in his arms. It would only be a few days, he told himself, but he was going to miss her. "You think she would mind if I kidnapped you?"

"She might," Amelia admitted, snuggling closer. "But I wouldn't."

His heart turned over. He rubbed his nose against hers. "Merry Christmas, Miss Amelia."

"Merry Christmas, Ben," she said, and gave him a long kiss full of love, yet tinged with uncertainty. The combination put a lump of odd emotions in his throat, and Ben felt a knot of dread in his gut.

He was going to lose her.

The realization hit Ben right in the middle of Christmas dinner at his sister's house, and it hit him hard enough that he didn't eat another bite.

He was going to lose Amelia. It might not be this week. It might not be next, but if they kept moving in the same direction, he was going to lose her. Ben believed Amelia loved him for himself as he'd never been loved before, but she was the kind of woman who would ultimately need commitment and marriage. Ben had always been firm on the subject of marriage. *Never.*

It had been an easy stance to take. No woman had

ever made him think past tomorrow. Amelia was different.

He tried to imagine his daily grind without Amelia, and felt a stab of pain that didn't go away. She was sunshine and peace to him. He was convinced she was the most compassionate, intelligent woman in the universe, and it never ceased to amaze him that she believed he was the most clever, special man on the face of the earth. She made him *feel* clever and special.

Ben had the sinking sense that he had gone and done it this time. He was in over his head. He was in love with Amelia, and he didn't know what to do about it.

Lost in thought for most of the afternoon, he gave a vague greeting to Stan and Jenna Jean when they popped in for a quick visit.

"What'd you do?" Stan asked as he joined Ben on the sofa. "Wreck your Harley?"

Ben shook his head and chuckled. "No. I'm okay. Just got a little something on my mind."

"Uh-oh. Sounds like woman trouble. I never thought I'd see the day."

"Merry Christmas to you, too," Ben said with a scowl.

Stan laughed and thumped Ben on the back. "It just proves you're human. I went through my share of it with Jenna."

Ben watched Stan glance at his wife with contentment in his eyes. Then he turned back to Ben. "Is she pregnant?"

"Hell, no!" Ben nearly yelled, making Jenna's head turn. He gave a grimace. "No," he said again, more quietly.

Stan shrugged. "Hey, if it happened to Joey, it can

happen to any of us. Did you get pictures of the baby in your Christmas card?''

Ben nodded, feeling an odd twist as he thought of the photo of their longtime buddy Joey with his wife and baby. "They looked happy."

"You gonna marry her?" Stan asked.

Ben shook his head. "I'm not the marrying kind."

Stan chuckled. "Ben, *none* of us are the marrying kind until we meet the right woman. But if Amelia doesn't make you want to take her home and keep her forever, then she's not the right woman. If you don't feel like life without her would be miserable, then she's not the right woman. If you don't love her, then—"

"Enough Stan." Ben glowered at his friend. He felt all those things and more for Amelia. "What's your point?"

"Humility is the beginning of wisdom," Stan said in a dry tone.

Ben leaned forward and propped his elbows on his knees. "She doesn't think I'm marriage material."

"You're not," Stan agreed.

Ben tossed him a sideways glance.

"But it wouldn't take much to make you marriage material. You can keep your Harley and your leather jacket. You just need to convince *her* that you're marriage material. You need a steady job," Stan said, lifting his index finger for the first on a list.

"I got an offer to sell the dealership," Ben interjected.

"Are you going to take it?"

Ben still felt torn. The offer would enable him to do something he'd always wanted to do. Would he have to choose between selling his dealership and losing Amelia? "I haven't decided."

Stan gave a low whistle. "Then you've got some tough decisions to make. If you want to keep her, if you really want to keep her, then you need to be someone she can count on."

Ben had always made sure women knew *not* to count on him. He shook his head. "I don't know about this."

"It's up to you. The right woman can bring you more happiness than you ever dreamed possible, or she can make you miserable as hell. It takes a lot of guts to make a commitment."

"Guts or insanity," Ben muttered.

"Then let her move on to someone who will commit," Stan said with a shrug. "You'll get over her."

Ben's stomach twisted violently at the notion of Amelia finding someone new. He felt possessive in all the ways that would make her call him a caveman. Getting over her didn't look easy. He rubbed his face and swore under his breath.

"Still not sure," Stan said. "Well, *if* you decide to keep her, you need a steady job...a willingness to watch chick flicks every now and then is helpful...be ready to kiss your bathroom goodbye. But most importantly, you just need to be so crazy in love with her that you can't imagine life without her. A ring and proposal are standard operating procedure."

Ben groaned. "Is that all?"

"A suit," Stan said, "for special occasions."

Appalled, Ben stared at him. "Special occasions!"

"Yeah. Weddings, anniversaries, baby christenings."

"My funeral," Ben said. "The only reason I'd need a suit is for my own funeral."

Four agonizing days later Ben stood in his office wearing a navy blue Brooks Brothers suit. One of his employees knocked on his door.

"Mr. Palmer—" The salesman faltered, then cleared his throat. "Excuse me, sir. Are condolences in order?"

Ben might have laughed if he hadn't been asked the same question by three other employees. "Nobody died. You had a question?"

"I, uh, wondered," the salesman said doubtfully, "if I could leave early tonight."

"How many salesmen do we have on the lot tonight?"

"Four, sir."

"Take off," Ben said, glancing at his own watch, wondering when Amelia would arrive. She'd called earlier and asked if she could meet him at the dealership instead of her house. Ben had changed into his suit just thirty minutes ago, and he already felt like he was wearing a straitjacket.

He had spent the week wrestling with his thoughts and feelings and had come to the conclusion that he could give up many things in his life, but Amelia wasn't one of them. He picked up the letter of intent from his prospective buyer and ripped it in half.

Another knock sounded at his door, making him instantly tense. "Yes," he said.

"Mr. Palmer, there's a customer in the lobby to see you." His sales manager raised his eyebrows. "We've got a live one."

Impatient, Ben tossed the torn papers on his desk. "Does it have to be me?"

"Oh, yeah. The customer's pretty insistent."

Swearing under his breath, he strode to the lobby and came to a screeching halt when he saw THE CUSTOMER. Dressed in curve-skimming black leather from her neck to her toes, she tugged off her motorcycle helmet and her curly brown hair fell over her shoulders.

Ben heard a muffled male moan when she lifted a hand to push a lock from her face. The gesture emphasized the slight bounce of her shapely breasts. Her cheeks were windblown pink, her lips arched in a nervous smile.

Every male eye in the showroom was on her, but she only had eyes for Ben.

"Hey, stud," she said with a cheeky grin. "I would ask you to go for a ride on my new bike, but you're not dressed for it."

Ben closed the distance between them and dipped his head. "New bike?"

She nodded. "I bought it today."

Feeling everyone's gaze on them, he took her hand, when he wanted to kiss her senseless. "Let's go to my office."

"Okay." She touched his coat sleeve as she walked beside him. "This is a beautiful suit, Ben. Who died?"

He heard a chorus of snickers among his employees and swore under his breath. "Nobody. Nobody died."

He pulled her into the office and his arms. As he shut the door, he took her mouth.

Amelia felt a soft sound of pleasure bubble from her throat. He felt warm and solid and alive. "I missed you," she whispered, wrapping herself around him.

"I missed you," he said, kissing her again. He pulled back to look at her. "What's with the leather?" he asked, sliding his hand down her hip possessively. "Why the new motorcycle?"

Amelia took a deep breath and fought an attack of nerves. "I decided I should become better equipped if you're going to take off on your cross-country tour." She watched him carefully. "I was hoping you might think about letting me go with you."

Ben stood stock-still.

Amelia's heart leaped into her throat. "Of course, it might take me some time to get up to speed," she added quickly, still waiting for him to respond.

"And I understand if you would want me to ride for only part of the trip...." She prayed for him to say something.

He swallowed audibly and lifted his hand to her cheek. Out of the corner of her eye, she saw his fingers tremble slightly.

"You bought a bike so you could ride cross-country with me?"

Amelia couldn't breathe. She bit her lip. "It was probably presumptuous, but you're—" she broke off, horrified by the threat of tears "—you're important to me. But if it's an imposition—"

"Oh, Lord, Amelia," he said, shaking his head, sliding his fingers through her hair. He rested his forehead against hers. "I want you to impose yourself on me in every possible way."

Amelia slumped in relief, her heart beating again. A tear squeezed out of the corner of her eye. "Oh, Ben." Another tear followed, then another.

Ben put his finger under her chin. "Sweetheart, why are you crying?"

She gulped. "I just love you. I love you too much."

He shook his head. "Never. Never too much." He tenderly kissed her. "I didn't sell the dealership."

She sniffed. "Why? I thought you wanted to ride cross-country."

He chuckled. "I wanted something else more. You see, I've got to convince a very special lady to stick with me."

Amelia frowned in confusion. "Stick with you?"

"Yeah, Amelia. I want you to stick with me. I love you," he said.

Amelia felt light-headed.

"That's the reason for the suit," Ben said.

"The suit?"

"So you'll think I'm marriage material," he said tightly.

Her knees felt weak. Amelia stared at him in shock. "Did you say m-m-marriage?"

"Yes."

"I'm going to fall," she said.

Ben propped her on the desk. His eyes adored her. "You are the best thing that's ever happened to me. I love you."

Overwhelmed, Amelia gave a tiny shake of her head. "I came in here trying to persuade you to take me on a road trip."

He leaned closer, stepping between her legs and meshing his body with hers. "I want more than a road trip, Amelia. I want you for life."

She still struggled with her doubts. "I will love you even if you don't marry me," she told him.

"Will you marry me?" he asked against her lips.

She gave the only answer she could. "Yes."

"I'll make your life crazy," he warned her, pulling off her jacket.

She smiled. "Good."

"Starting now," he continued and unfastened her leather pants.

Her heart kicked into triple time. "You started making me crazy a long time ago." When he slid his hands beneath her shirt and boldly cupped her breasts, she gasped. "Ben, what are you doing?"

He swept the top of his desk clean with one swift movement from his hand. "I'm making love to the woman I'm going to marry."

Her stomach dipped. "Oh, wow. I'm way over my quota for doing scary things today."

Ben chuckled. "You and me both, darlin'."

He kissed her, and Amelia melted into a puddle of sunshine. She awkwardly pulled at his new suit, and he tugged off her clothes. Breathless moments passed and she urged him closer. She couldn't get enough of his mouth, of his touch, of his body taking hers. She couldn't get enough of him.

"Inside," she whispered. "Come inside."

Ben groaned. "Protection," he muttered.

"I've taken care of it," Amelia told him, wrapping her legs around his back.

He held her hips and thrust inside her, his gaze never wavering from hers. The power of his love branded her body, mind and soul. He pumped in a mind-robbing, heart-throbbing rhythm. She jerked and slid over the top, savoring the pleasure, exulting in the passion on Ben's face.

He shattered inside her, murmuring her name again and again. Propping himself on his arms, he surrounded her with his body. "Oh, Amelia, don't ever stop loving me too much."

Epilogue

They said it wouldn't last. But it did.

On a sunny afternoon in May, Ben and Amelia thumbed their noses at all the naysayers by promising to love each other forever. The naysayers didn't mind the nose thumbing too much, Ben thought as he glanced at the happy crowd. They were too busy congratulating him, eating wedding cake and drinking champagne.

From across the room, Ben watched his bride and felt his heart swell with love and pride. Amelia was dressed in cream-colored lace with her hair wild and curly just the way he liked it. Her friends made admiring sounds over the unusual ring of diamonds and pearls he'd had specially designed for her. He remembered when he'd given it to her she'd cried so hard that it had alarmed him, until she'd made it clear they were tears of joy.

Too happy to buck convention, Ben had worn a tux during the ceremony and reception. Now he was back in his jacket and jeans, his tolerance of the social aspect of weddings at an end.

Ben wanted his bride's undivided attention.

Catching her gaze, he walked toward her. Her eyes widened at his change in attire. She smiled. "Tux get a little uncomfortable?"

"No," Ben said, sliding his hands around her waist. "It's time to go."

"Time to go," Maddie said, stepping forward when she overheard him. "Don't you think you're rushing things a little?"

"No." He swung Amelia into his arms, and she gave a surprised little squeal. "Say good-night, everybody. I'm kidnapping my wife."

A rush of contagious laughter swept over the crowd.

"Are you sure that bow tie didn't cut off your circulation?" Amelia asked, her cheeks high with color.

He met her gaze. "I've been a very generous man," he said, "sharing you with all these people for most of the day."

"You couldn't feel greedy about me," she said, delight shining in her eyes. "Not when you're going to be stuck with me forever."

"I guess I'm just gonna have to show you," Ben said in a mock long-suffering voice.

"But what about the throwing of the bouquet?" Amelia's mother demanded.

Ben gave his new mother-in-law a quick kiss on the cheek and kept moving. "Better hurry if you want a shot at catching the flowers," he called.

With a flock of unattached women in pursuit, Ben

carried Amelia to his motorcycle and started it. He wrapped his arm around her waist while he waited for her to throw the bouquet. From the back of his bike, she tossed them high in the air.

"One more promise," Amelia said, breathlessly turning back to him.

"Anything," he said, staring into her eyes, still amazed by the love they shared.

"I want you to promise that you will keep kidnapping me for the rest of my life."

"I will," Ben said, and he and his bride rode off into the sunshine together.

* * * * *

SILHOUETTE® *Desire* ®

THE RULE BREAKERS

an exciting new series by
Leanne Banks

Meet The Rulebreakers: A millionaire, a bad boy, a protector. Three strong, sexy men who take on the ultimate challenge—love!

Coming in September 1998—MILLIONAIRE DAD

Joe Caruthers had it all. Who would have thought that a brainy beauty like Marley Fuller—pregnant with his child—would cause this bachelor with everything to take the plunge?

Coming in October 1998—
THE LONE RIDER TAKES A BRIDE

Bad boy Ben Palmer had rebelled against falling in love, until he took the lovely, sad-eyed Amelia Russell on a moonlit ride.

Coming in November 1998—THIRTY-DAY FIANCÉ

Nick Nolan had to pretend to be engaged to his childhood friend Olivia Polnecek. Why was Nick noticing how perfect a wife she could be—for real!

Available at your favorite retail outlet.

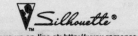

Silhouette ®

Take 2 bestselling love stories FREE
Plus get a FREE surprise gift!

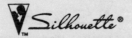

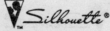

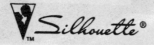

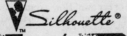

COMING NEXT MONTH

#1177 SLOW TALKIN' TEXAN—Mary Lynn Baxter
Ornery Porter Wyman, November's *Man of the Month*, was married
to his Texas fortune, but money couldn't mother his baby boy. Sexy,
nurturing Ellen Saxton...now, *she* could raise a child. *And* this single
father's desire...for marriage?

#1178 HER HOLIDAY SECRET—Jennifer Greene
Her past twenty-four hours were a total blank! By helping elusive beauty
Maggie Fletcher regain her lost day, small-town sheriff Andy Gautier was
in danger of losing his *bachelorhood*. But would Maggie's holiday secret
prevent her from becoming this lawman's Christmas bride?

#1179 THIRTY-DAY FIANCÉ—Leanne Banks
The Rulebreakers

Tough-as-nails Nick Nolan was lovely Olivia Polnecek's childhood
protector. Now *she* was coming to *his* rescue by posing as his fiancée.
She'd always dreamed of wearing Nick's ring, sleeping in his arms. So
playing "devoted" was easy—and all part of her plan to turn their thirty-
day engagement into a thirty-*year* marriage....

**#1180 THE OLDEST LIVING MARRIED VIRGIN—
Maureen Child**
The Bachelor Battalion

When innocent Donna Candello was caught tangled in Jack Harris's
bedsheets, the honorable marine married her in name only. But their
compromising position hadn't actually *compromised* Donna Candello
at all...and the oldest living married virgin's first wedded task was to
convince her new husband to give his blushing bride somethin' to
blush about!

#1181 THE RE-ENLISTED GROOM—Amy J. Fetzer
Seven years ago levelheaded Maxie Parrish shocked rough-'n'-reckless
Sergeant Kyle Hayden, leaving *him* at the altar. And nine months later
Maxie had a surprise of her own! Now a certain never-forgotten ex-fiancé
appeared at Maxie's ranch rarin' to round up the wife that got away...but
what of the daughter he never knew?

#1182 THE FORBIDDEN BRIDE-TO-BE—Kathryn Taylor
Handsome, wealthy Alex Sinclair was Sophie Anders's perfect marriage
match. Problem was, she already had a fiancé—his brother! True, her
engagement was a phony, but the baby she was carrying was for real—
and belonged to Alex. Once Sophie began to "show," would Alex make
their forbidden affair into a wedded forever after?